At the crest of the mountain, they dismounted, tied their horses to trees, and went the rest of the way on foot. Once on the flat rock of the plateau, the three of them fanned out to search for the tepee of twigs Lacey had tied together to form the memorial.

"Over here!" Katie called. "I found it."

Chelsea and Lacey hurried to where Katie was crouched, digging through a pile of dead leaves. The tepee was partially buried, and Chelsea held her breath, hoping that the laminated photo and Jillian's diamond stud earring were still tied to it.

"It's come apart," Katie said, lifting up the twigs in three parts. But from the corner of one of the sticks, the laminated photo dangled, and from its center the diamond caught the afternoon sunlight.

The photo looked faded, but Amanda still smiled from the center of their group. Chelsea felt a lump form in her throat. These days, she and Katie and Lacey looked older, more mature, healthier too. But Amanda looked the same, her gamine smile frozen in time. And ageless.

Katie took the photo from Lacey's trembling fingers. "We were quite a bunch, weren't we?"

ONE LAST WISH

Lurlene McDaniel

A Season for Goodbye

BANTAM BOOKS

NEW YORK • TORONTO • LONDON • SYDNEY • AUCKLAND

RL 5, age 10 and up

A SEASON FOR GOODBYE
A Bantam Book / April 1995

ISBN 0-553-56265-7

Published simultaneously in the United States and Canada

Bantam Books are published by Bantam Books, a division of Random
House, Inc Its trademark, consisting of the words "Bantam Books" and
the portrayal of a rooster, is Registered in U S Patent and Trademark
Office and in other countries Marca Registrada Bantam Books, 1540
Broadway, New York, New York 10036

PRINTED IN THE UNITED STATES OF AMERICA

OPM   19   18   17   16   15   14

This book is dedicated
to all my faithful readers.
Thank you for your support and loyalty.
You're the greatest!

One

❦

"KATIE O'ROARK, YOU look fab!" Chelsea James said, throwing her arms around her good friend. "I'm glad you're here with me. I'm sort of scared about this whole thing," Chelsea whispered into Katie's ear.

"Scared of being a counselor at Jenny House?" Katie's eyebrows shot up in surprise. "Chelsea, don't be ridiculous. You've come through a heart transplant and are doing fine. This will be a piece of cake!"

"I'm only a counselor-in-training," Chelsea corrected, pulling away. "I couldn't believe it when Mr. Holloway wrote and invited me. You know the only reason I agreed was because I'd get to spend the summer with you and Lacey again." Chelsea glanced around the nearly empty lobby of Jenny House. The counselors and trainees had arrived three days early for orientation and most had gone upstairs to unpack before the first meeting. "Where is Lacey anyway?"

Katie shrugged. "You know she runs on Laceytime, not daylight saving time. She'll be here eventually."

"Is it true that Jeff McKensie's coming with her? I couldn't believe it when she wrote to say that they were together. I mean, she avoided him like the plague last year."

Katie almost told Chelsea that getting back together with Jeff was mostly Lacey's idea, but decided to let Lacey tell her if she wanted her to know. "I think her stint in the hospital last spring when her diabetes went out of control caused Lacey to reevaluate some things," Katie said.

"She *is* okay now, isn't she?"

"She says she is, but . . ." Katie let the sentence trail because she wasn't sure how Lacey was actually doing. She only had Lacey's offhanded reports to go on, and Lacey often said she was fine when she wasn't.

"But you're feeling good, aren't you?" Chelsea asked. "You look a little tense."

Katie assured Chelsea that she was in great health, knowing that it was important to her friend. After all, they'd both had heart transplants and Chelsea tended to gauge her own health by the standard of Katie's. She flashed Chelsea a quick smile, hoping to cover up the tension her friend had so astutely picked up on. The trouble with Chelsea was that she was too darn intuitive. "I've just got a lot on my mind. I've been offered a track scholarship to Arizona."

"You have? That's super. I know how badly you wanted one. So I guess you'll head out there after Jenny House's summer session is over."

Katie was tempted to tell Chelsea the truth about the strain the offer was putting on her relationship with her parents and Josh. "I'm undecided," she said.

Chelsea's eyes widened. "But it's what you've always wanted."

Katie wished she'd not said anything. Standing in the lobby before a meeting wasn't the place to unburden her heart—not even to one of her best friends. Fortunately, the main door swung open and Lacey Duval breezed inside, followed by two members of the staff lugging her belongings. After shrieks and hugs, Katie eyed the encumbered staff personnel and declared, "Good grief, Lacey, you could stock a small department store. We're only supposed to be here twelve weeks."

"I couldn't decide what to bring, so I brought it all."

"Where do we take this stuff?" one of the burdened staffers asked.

"Third floor," Katie told him. "Room 17. Lacey, we're across the hall from each other and Chelsea's next door to me. You two will have two kids apiece in your rooms with you. I get three."

"It's not quite like last year," Chelsea said with a nervous laugh. Katie had been in charge of their room the summer before. That's where they'd all met for the first time. Amanda had been with them then.

When Amanda died, they all felt the loss and grief but the experience had cemented their friendship. Their different backgrounds, medical problems, and ages didn't matter.

"Where's Jeff?" Chelsea strained to see through the tinted glass doors to the sunlit wooden deck.

"He's parking the car."

"Your mom let you drive up here alone with him all the way from Miami?" Chelsea asked.

"Don't worry. The trip was harmless. We spent the night with an aunt of mine in Savannah. We left Savannah this morning and might have gotten here sooner if Jeff hadn't insisted we eat lunch and loaf around a few rest stops." She rolled her eyes. "Ever since I got out of the hospital he treats me like I might break or something."

"You scared us all," Katie insisted. "Even when I saw you in Miami during the national track championships in March, you looked thin."

Lacey spun, showing off her shape in her jeans and T-shirt. "How do I look now?"

"Better," Katie admitted. In truth, Katie thought Lacey looked terrific. Her long blond hair was streaked with sunny highlights and her skin glowed with a warm golden hue. And she had added some much-needed weight.

The front door swung open and in sauntered Jeff, his arm slung around the neck of a tall redheaded guy. "Hey, look who I found in the parking lot. He's helping out here this summer like we are."

"Josh!" Lacey and Chelsea cried in unison. Lacey

eyed Katie. "This *is* a surprise. You didn't let on Josh was coming with you."

Josh intervened by saying, "She didn't know. I sort of wrote Mr. Holloway and invited myself to be on staff. I'll be working with the groundspeople and helping out in the kitchen."

"Cool," Jeff said with a grin. "Now I have a buddy and I won't have to listen to all that female screeching by myself."

"Screeching?" Lacey said icily. "I can arrange it so that you don't have to listen to *anything*."

Josh stepped between Lacey and Jeff, making a mock play at shielding Jeff's body with his. "Run for it, Jeff. I'll cover you."

Everyone but Katie broke out laughing. She simply took a step backward and turned her attention toward the massive portrait of Jenny Crawford hanging over the soaring stone fireplace. "Anything wrong?" Lacey wanted to know.

"Nothing," Katie said tightly. She refused to meet Josh's gaze as he stood beside Lacey, his smile fading into an expression of hurt.

His expression stabbed at her. She was being hateful and she knew it, but she couldn't seem to help herself. The announcement that he was joining her at Jenny House for the summer had jolted her. She'd been counting on the time away from him to seriously think about their future together.

Jeff broke the awkward moment by saying, "Help me take my stuff upstairs, Josh, before the meeting starts. I can smell pizza and I'm starved."

"You just ate two hours ago," Lacey said.

"Is there a rule about my stomach punching a time clock?"

She reached out and squeezed his midriff. "If I can pinch more than an inch, you'll have to diet."

He retaliated by patting her flat torso. "And if I *can't* grab more than an inch, you've got to eat more." She opened her mouth but before she could speak, he added, "Doctor's orders."

Lacey made a face at him, but acquiesced, which surprised Katie. She'd expected a sharp comeback. Maybe Lacey was turning over a new leaf in order to win back Jeff.

The guys left the lobby for the parking lot and Lacey asked, "So, who's going to help me unpack?"

Chelsea volunteered. "Katie, you coming too?"

"If it's okay, I think I'll go for a little jog. I feel cooped up from the ride in the car and need to stretch my legs."

Lacey wrinkled her pretty, turned-up nose. "Ugh. You physical fitness nuts are all alike."

"Catch you later," Katie said, stepping backward and starting for the door. She was outside in the warm North Carolina afternoon before Lacey or Chelsea could say another word. She loped off the deck, down the wooden stairs, and out onto a trail leading away from Jenny House and into the cool, leafy woods. In minutes, she found her stride and settled into the familiar surroundings.

You need to run, she told herself. She needed time alone. Needed time to think. She was just beginning to mull over her dilemma when she heard someone calling her name from behind her. Katie stopped, pivoted, and saw Josh coming toward her, his long legs making short work of the distance.

She tensed as he approached. He stopped in front of her, and for a moment the sound of their breathing was all that filled the air of the deep, green woods. He cocked his head, looking down at her. A stubborn thatch of red hair spilled over his forehead and his blue eyes looked troubled. "I thought you were helping Jeff," she said.

"I saw you take off and told Jeff I needed to talk to you."

"We've said it all, Josh. What's left to talk about?"

"I love you, Katie," he said softly. "And I can't stand it when you're mad at me. Can't you forgive me for signing on at Jenny House this summer? Can't we be together like we used to be?"

Two

MEMORIES SPILLED THROUGH Katie as she gazed at Josh's face. She saw him as he'd been two years before, looking scared and uncertain in the rec room of the hospital while she sat alone in a wheelchair, recuperating from her heart transplant operation. She saw him as he'd looked at her then, longing to touch her —more than her—to touch his brother, whose heart beat inside her chest.

She saw him as he'd been that night in the moonlight before she'd run in the Transplant Olympic Games. The first time he'd kissed her. The night he'd given her the golden heart pendant necklace she always wore around her neck. She saw him coaching her, helping her to run again, to regain her speed and fitness. For the past two years of her life there had only been Josh, her first serious boyfriend. Her first love.

Katie felt her pent-up anger and hostility toward him dissipate. In a soft pleading tone, she said, "How can I make you understand that going away to college isn't breaking things off with you?"

"And why can't you understand that I'm afraid if you go away, you won't come back?"

"I'll come back."

"Heart transplant recipients have a solid five-year track record. You already have two of those years behind you. If you go away, the next three will pass without me."

"Plenty of heart transplant patients live longer than five years," she insisted, sensing her frustration rebuilding. "How can you put a time limit on my life? That's not for you to say."

"I'm not trying to limit you. I'm trying to make the most of the time you have. I want to marry you, Katie. Have you forgotten I've asked you?"

"Of course not."

"If you stay in Ann Arbor and start classes at Michigan like I'll be doing, we can spend more time together, make wedding plans. Gramps thinks it's a good idea. He wants to see me get married, get settled, because he's getting old and you know his health isn't so good."

She felt a twinge of guilt. Josh and his grandfather had done so much for her. Given her so much. Still she knew she had dreams of her own that preceded her meeting Josh. "But to run track for an NCAA school is something I've dreamed about all my life.

When my heart pooped out, before I had the transplant, I thought that dream was gone. Now it's been given back to me." She clutched Josh's hands. "Don't you see? I'll never have this chance again."

"You can run for Michigan. They have a great women's track team."

Frustration gave way to exasperation. "But at Arizona I have the opportunity to be completely on my own. To live like a regular person."

Josh's gaze bore into her. "And regular people date other people."

"Is that what you think? That I want to move away so that I can date somebody else?"

"I was with you during the school year. I know what happened between you and Garrison Reilly."

Katie's exasperation erupted into anger. "Give it a rest, Josh—*nothing* happened between me and Garrison. How many times do I have to tell you that?"

"That wasn't Garrison's story."

Josh's statement caused Katie to gape in surprise. The memory of Garrison's Christmas party surfaced, and of Josh taking her, then getting angry and leaving her stranded. Garrison had danced with her, held her close, and kissed her under mistletoe. The feelings he kindled had frightened her, and ever since that night she'd avoided Garrison purposely. "What did he say? And when?"

"Guys talk," Josh said. "Things get said in the locker room. It was no secret that he wanted to date you."

"But I didn't date him. And now I'm here at Jenny House for the summer and he's back in Ann Arbor."

"But if he was here, would you date him?" Josh's jaw jutted stubbornly.

His jealous prodding was the final straw. Katie erupted with, "I can't believe we're having this conversation! This is exactly why I wanted to be off by myself this summer. And to some extent, why I want to go away to college. I need breathing space."

"Oh, so now I'm smothering you. Is that it?"

"What you're doing is making me furious!" Katie stamped her foot. "This discussion is terminated." She spun and started running deeper into the woods. Fury and frustration drove her, and soon her heart was pounding and her breath came in gasps. She finally stopped and leaned against a tree for support. Her legs felt wobbly. She struggled to calm herself, knowing that stress was throwing her off her stride and taking its toll physically.

Katie slid to the ground, pulled her knees tightly against her body, and buried her face in her hands. How had her life gotten so complicated? Why couldn't she just go away to college, and run track, and study physical education, and have a good time?

Automatically, her hand slid over her left breast to feel the thudding rhythm of the organ buried inside her chest. *My heart,* she thought. No . . . not *her* heart at all. Aaron's heart. Josh's brother. Josh and Gramps had given her an irreplaceable gift. She was simply a vessel for it. A caretaker.

"I *do* love Josh," she whispered out loud. "I really do." She waited while tears slid down her cheeks unchecked, grateful that there was no one to hear her weeping except the trees and the sky.

*   *   *

By the time Katie returned to Jenny House, she had less than thirty minutes to shower and dress for the get-acquainted meeting. The lobby area bustled with activity and she was surprised at how many more people she saw this year compared to last. But then, last summer Jenny House had been an experiment, a dream of Richard Holloway's. From the looks of things, his dream was going to be successful, Katie thought as she hurried to the elevator.

As the doors opened, a woman stepped off, almost colliding with Katie. "Oops," the woman said. "Sorry, I didn't mean to knock you over." She extended her hand and Katie shook it, noticing that the woman, though tall and attractive and athletic-looking, had only one arm. "Kimbra Patterson. I've come to help with sports and physical fitness."

Inadvertently, Katie's gaze went to the empty sleeve. She blushed furiously when Kimbra said, "Don't let this fool you—I'm pretty athletic without it. I lost my arm to cancer when I was fourteen, so I've learned to make do without it. I play a pretty mean game of tennis." She grinned. "How about you? Would you like to meet me on the courts some morning?"

"I've never played much tennis," Katie said.

"No problem. That's why I'm here—to help anybody learn who wants to. And Mr. Holloway thought I'd be an inspiration because so many kids with health problems think they're handicapped for sports and they're not."

Katie thought of Chelsea, whose heart problems had robbed her of a normal life. "Maybe my friends and I might give you a match," Katie said.

A quick smile from Kimbra, and, "Good. Now, don't let me keep you. You look as if you were in a hurry."

"I am. I don't want to be late for the meeting." She started into the elevator. "By the way, my name's Katie."

"I know who you are."

"You do?" Katie halted the door from closing. "How do you know me?"

"You are one of the people who've received Wish money.

"Yes. Did you?"

Kimbra smiled. "Let's just say I knew all about One Last Wish before it ever became One Last Wish."

"But how—"

"We'll talk later." Kimbra backed away. "I don't want to make you late."

Alone on the elevator, Katie puzzled over the friendly but mysterious Kimbra. What had she meant? *Things sure are different this summer*, she told herself. Now, if she could just get things sorted out with Josh. Recalling Josh and their argument made Katie sigh. What she really wanted this summer was to be around her friends. And take time to think about her future. Josh shouldn't have invited himself to come help out at Jenny House.

It wasn't going to be easy to make decisions about her tomorrows with him trying to persuade her to his way of thinking. Katie hurried to her room, forcing everything out of her mind except the idea of a hot shower and the meeting ahead of her. She also had a job to do at Jenny House. Just like last summer. Kids were coming who might not even be alive in another year's time. Katie was determined to help out every way she could.

And because Josh had helped give her a second chance at living, she promised herself that she would be good to him. Because she loved him. And she owed him. Big time.

Three

"Which one should I wear?" Lacey asked, holding up two equally trendy outfits for Chelsea to evaluate. Her friend had stretched out on one of the beds in Lacey's room.

"Jeez—it's only a get-acquainted meeting. What does it matter what you wear?" Suitcases and duffel bags, clothes spilling out, were strewn across every flat surface. Chelsea had put her things away in less than thirty minutes and come into Lacey's room in order to prod her along.

"It matters," Lacey said with a toss of her silky blond hair. "Jeff will be there and I want him to see me at my best."

Chelsea puckered up her face. "What's the big deal? He's already nuts about you."

"Um—that might not be the case," Lacey admitted, holding the pieces against her body and checking herself out in the bureau mirror.

Chelsea sat upright. "What do you mean? I thought you and he were Siamese twins. What haven't you told me?"

"I sort of blew it between us this past school year. When he transferred to the University of Miami in January, he tried to start things up between us, but I acted stupid and dumped him."

"Why?"

"Temporary insanity." Lacey tossed one of the outfits on the bed and slipped into the bathroom to dress. She continued her story through the half-closed bathroom door. "Actually, I thought I liked some jerk in my school, but Todd was a real waste of time. Honestly, it wasn't even Todd that I wanted as much as the chance to be in the right crowd and forget all about my diabetes."

Lacey emerged from the bathroom and rummaged through a makeup kit sitting atop the bureau. "As you may remember, I've never been a fan of having diabetes."

"*That's* an understatement." Chelsea recalled the belligerent Lacey from the previous summer and how she hated being forced to come to Jenny House. And although she had finally become friends and had fun at the House, Lacey's dislike of her disease hadn't improved when she returned home. "Is that why you messed up your control and ended up in the hospital?" Chelsea asked. "Trying to impress Todd and his friends?"

"Listen, I've spent hours with a shrink at the Diabetes Research Institute and I've learned that Todd was only one part of my screwy outlook. My warring parents were in the picture too."

"And now that they're divorced, things are all right?"

"As good as they'll ever be." Lacey waved her hand impatiently. "It's old news. I only know that one day I woke up and realized that Jeff was what I wanted."

"And now you're telling me that he's no longer interested in you? It didn't seem that way in the lobby. I mean, the two of you drove together all the way from Miami."

"A trip of polite togetherness. Very brotherly." Lacey made a face. "He doesn't trust me not to dump him again."

"Because he's a hemophiliac?" Chelsea remembered Lacey's aversion to every kind of illness—not just her own.

"I guess that's part of it."

"Well, how *do* you feel? What would you do if he had to go in for transfusions?"

"I wouldn't walk out on him," Lacey insisted. But Chelsea wasn't absolutely convinced. Lacey had a mind of her own and she did what she wanted, even if it hurt someone's feelings.

"Is that why you decided to help out at Jenny House this summer? Just to be near Jeff?"

Lacey whirled. "Chelsea, what a mean thing to say! I came because I really want to help."

Chelsea's face reddened. "I didn't mean to imply you had an ulterior motive."

"Also, I came because I wanted to spend time with

you and Katie. And because I didn't want to hang around home all summer with nothing to do while Mom works. Plus she's dating some guy, so I thought I'd give her a break and stay out of her way. She'll have a better time without worrying about tripping over me."

Lacey smiled and flapped her eyelashes. "But I won't lie—Jeff's working here *is* an additional perk for me. Enough about me. How's your love life?"

Chelsea laugh mirthlessly. "What love life?" She sighed and stretched back onto the bed. "I thought that once I got my transplant and started attending school regularly, I'd be a regular person. But during the school year I discovered that everybody already had best friends. And ran with certain crowds. No matter how hard I tried, I felt like an outsider all year long. I learned that there wasn't any place for me. Especially with the guys."

"How about Jillian's brother? What was his name? I remember you liked him."

"DJ," Chelsea supplied. "He lives in Texas, and besides things were always awkward between us—especially after I got the transplant and his sister died." She didn't add that DJ already had a girlfriend and hadn't even noticed Chelsea's existence except for when his sister forced him to interact with her.

"But that wasn't your fault."

"Let's just drop it, all right? I'll never see DJ again anyway." It pained Chelsea to say it, but she knew it was true. All the years she was sick, she'd kept to herself, with her parents, tutors, and books being her main source of friendships. Coming to Jenny House last summer had been the best change. A world she'd never been able to be a part of before had opened up. Then, living with Katie and her family in Michigan, and meeting Jillian in the transplant program, had made her have hope. Getting the heart transplant and surviving had given Chelsea a brand-new life. Her crush on DJ had been especially thrilling. Then Jillian had died. Chelsea wasn't completely over the loss of her friend even now—months afterward.

"Things will improve for you next school year," Lacey said as she put on lipstick. "And who knows? Maybe you'll meet someone here this summer."

Chelsea doubted it. But it wasn't going to be easy hanging around with Lacey and Katie when they both had boyfriends. She sighed, feeling again like an outsider. "Where is Katie anyway? She should have been back from that run by now."

"I saw Josh take off after her. I'm sure they had some things to iron out," Lacey said.

"What things? Don't tell me there's trouble in paradise. I mean, Katie and Josh are an institution."

Lacey busied herself with brushing her already perfectly sleek hair. "Did I say there was trouble?"

Chelsea wasn't reassured. And she felt even more isolated. When she'd lived with Katie they'd talked about everything. But once she'd returned home, letters and occasional phone calls were all they'd had to bridge the distance. Obviously, something had happened between Josh and Katie that Lacey knew about and that Katie had failed to share with Chelsea. "I noticed some bad vibes between them in the lobby. What gives?"

Lacey never had a chance to answer because Katie swept into the room, her hair still damp from her shower. "Are you two ready?" she asked breathlessly. "We don't want to be late."

"Says who?" Lacey asked. "I think we should make a grand entrance."

"I think we should be on time," Katie countered.

Chelsea slid off the bed and stood between her two friends. "Incredibly, after forty-five minutes of nonstop effort, Lacey really is ready. And we were just wondering where you were. Come on, both of you, follow me."

Lacey took one final glance in the mirror and the three of them headed downstairs. In the lobby, a small crowd of staff, counselors, and kids in training to be counselors were gathered on the sofas and folding chairs in front of the fireplace. Richard Holloway, the director, stood in front of the massive stone hearth. Chelsea thought that he looked like a male model, tall, slim, and blond with impeccable clothing. Above him hung the massive painting of Jenny Crawford, the woman who started the One Last Wish Foundation and, according to Katie, Mr. Holloway's one true love.

"Welcome," Mr. Holloway said with a dazzling smile. "The pizza's waiting down in the rec room, so I'll make these comments brief."

A couple of boys clapped. Chelsea saw Josh standing with Jeff and wondered again what was going on.

Mr. Holloway continued. "We have lots of new

faces. Several who were attendees last year have returned to help others have a fun summer and I'm pleased about that. We'll break into small groups after we eat. Each group will be made up of a staff member, a returning counselor, and some new faces. Questions are welcome."

He placed his hands in his trouser pockets. "This year, we'll be taking on some attendees with specific medical problems—kids still taking chemo, which the medical staff will administrate. But some of you will have one of these chemo kids in your rooms and so you'll need specific instructions and details."

Beside her, Chelsea heard Lacey suck in her breath and instantly knew the problem. "Don't worry," she whispered. "I'm sure they won't give one of them to us first-timers."

Mr. Holloway discussed the ideals and purposes of Jenny House and was almost ready to move the group downstairs when the lobby door swung open and a muscular boy wearing cowboy boots and a Stetson hat rushed inside. "Sorry I'm late," he said in an unmistakable Texan drawl. "My flight's been circling the airport and didn't land on time."

"DJ Longado, welcome," Mr. Holloway said. "Everybody, this young man has volunteered to be in charge of the stables this summer. He'll be giving riding lessons and leading trail rides."

Chelsea barely heard the introduction. Her pulse had started pounding and all the blood had left her face. *DJ Longado.* The last person in the world she expected to ever see again.

Four

⤴⤵

"WELL, WHAT DO you know . . ." Lacey said, leveling a look at Chelsea when the group broke up for pizza. "And to think we were just talking about dear ole DJ. This sort of puts a new twist on your summer, doesn't it?"

Chelsea hung back, ignoring Lacey's needling.

"Give her a break," Katie said. Chelsea had discussed her feelings about DJ with Katie while she'd been recovering from her transplant operation, and so Katie was the one who understood how difficult seeing DJ was on Chelsea.

"What's the big deal?" Lacey asked. "If you like this guy, go after him."

"It's not that easy," Chelsea declared. "I—I'm not pretty and boys never notice me."

"I can fix that," Lacey insisted. "Remember how makeup improved Amanda? I can fix you up—"

"I'm not one of your makeovers, Lacey," Chelsea interrupted, stamping her foot.

"Well, excuse me. I was just trying to be helpful. You don't have to bite my head off."

Katie put her hand on Lacey's shoulder and gave her a gentle nudge. "Go on down and save us some pizza before Josh and Jeff eat their share and ours too. We'll be there in a few minutes."

Lacey swished off and Katie turned to Chelsea. "Come on. It'll be okay."

"No way. I can't go down there and face DJ."

"Why?"

"I—I'm embarrassed. Jillian probably told him I had a thing for him. I can't look him in the face."

"You can't avoid him all summer either."

"I keep remembering the last time I saw him, at the hospital. I felt so awful. I'd had the transplant, but Jillian couldn't get hers. I'll never forget the look DJ gave me. Like—like he hated me."

"That's not true," Katie said quickly. "His sister was dying. He just felt helpless. It had nothing to do with you."

Chelsea wasn't so sure. But Katie was right about not being able to avoid him all summer. They were both there together and sooner or later their paths would cross. "I never liked horseback riding anyway," Chelsea sighed. "I'll stay away from the stables altogether."

"You can't. Remember, we're supposed to ride up the ridge to the memorial we made for Amanda. I want to see if the photo's still there and if Jillian's earring is gone." Katie bent closer. "Maybe the fairies took it."

Chelsea smiled at Katie's attempt to perk her up. "I do want to go up there."

"Well, you can't go with us unless you check out a horse from the stable."

"You and Lacey could check one out for me and I could meet you farther up the trail." Chelsea gazed at Katie hopefully.

"We won't do it."

"I'd do it for you."

"I have an idea. Why don't you march right down to the rec room, go right up to DJ, give him your biggest smile, and tell him hello."

Chelsea shrank back. "I couldn't."

"Sure you can. Don't you know the best way to get over a rough spot is to face it head-on? I do it all the time when I compete. When I know I'll be facing an especially strong opponent, I walk up to her, smile, and say, 'Good luck.'" Katie chuckled. "It unnerves them. But taking the initiative gives me an edge. It'll work for you too."

"I'm scared."

"No, you're just nervous. I remember when you were afraid to do anything that made your heart beat faster. But you've come such a long way since last summer—why, you've made it through countless games of Virtual Reality *and* survived a heart transplant. Don't go back to that scaredy-cat mode. Especially over some guy."

Reluctantly, Chelsea followed Katie down to the

rec room, where the aroma of hot pizza permeated the air. Other kids were friendly to her, but she was so jittery she almost dropped her slice of pizza. Yet, once she'd regained control of the paper plate, she screwed up her courage and walked over to where DJ was sitting alone at a video game console. "Hi," she said brightly. "Remember me?"

"You're Chelsea," he said, but his gaze looked wary and not very friendly. "How're you doing?"

Her knees felt rubbery, so she sat at the tabletop console in the chair opposite him. "I'm doing fine. How about you?"

"I'm okay."

"And your mom and dad?"

"They're all right too."

Chelsea felt as if he was forcing himself to talk to her and she was dismayed. Why didn't he like her? She'd tried so hard to be nice to him. And she cared so much about him. "It's nice of you to come and help out here this summer," she said, trying again to be friendly. "It'll be good to have somebody who knows one end of a horse from the other." She ventured a smile.

"I came because I promised my sister I would," DJ said. "And a promise is a promise."

"You're doing this as a favor to Jillian?"

"Yeah. Something wrong with that?"

Chelsea felt her face flush crimson. "Oh, no! Of course not. It's just that . . . well . . . I wonder why she wanted you to." Her words came out quickly, then trailed off, like air running out of a balloon.

"Because she couldn't do it herself," DJ said tersely. He stood. "She'll never get to do any of the things she liked to do again. She'll never ride her horse, or finish school, or even grow up. She wanted to do all those things, you know."

"I—I know. She left me a videotape—"

"Well, she left me the job of coming here for the summer and helping out. So I came." His eyes had grown dark and his mouth compressed into a hard line. "Look, I haven't got time to stand around and talk. I came here to work and I plan to pretty much keep to myself. I'm going down to the stables and get acquainted with the horses."

"Sure, I understand . . ." Chelsea's sentence trickled off as DJ left the rec room. She felt small and humiliated and wished she could sink into the floor.

"What's up?" Katie asked, coming up and settling into DJ's chair.

"I was right—he hates me," Chelsea mumbled miserably.

"That's not so."

"Then tell me why he can't stand being in the same room with me. You didn't hear how cold he sounded when he talked to me. And you didn't see the look in his eyes. He'd rather go be with a bunch of horses than be near me."

Katie leaned forward. "He just doesn't feel comfortable, that's all. I mean, who does? We're all basically strangers."

But nothing Katie said could change Chelsea's mind. DJ disliked her, and forcing herself on him wasn't going to change his mind. "You remember that tape Jillian left me?" Chelsea asked.

Katie nodded. "You never shared it with anyone."

"I—I just never could." Chelsea glanced at Katie hesitantly. "You aren't angry with me because I never showed it to you, are you?"

"Of course not."

"Well, there's this one part where she asks me to look out for DJ for her." Chelsea gave a mirthless laugh. "As if he needs me or even wants me to."

"He may warm up as the summer moves along. I'm going to ask Josh and Jeff to make friends with him."

"But please don't tell them that I used to like him or anything."

"I won't."

Just then, Mr. Holloway announced that it was time to break up into small groups. He divided up the boys' floors first—a staff member for every returning counselor and two to three trainees for each group. When the girls were regrouped, Chelsea found herself in the same group with Katie and Lacey and a woman staffer named Kimbra, whom she didn't recall from the previous summer.

Kimbra Patterson was outgoing and friendly. Chelsea saw that Lacey was having a hard time ignoring that Kimbra only had one arm, but once she explained how she'd lost it to cancer and appeared so at ease with it, it became easier to overlook.

"We've got six campers to supervise," Kimbra explained, riffling through a professional-looking folder. "Three have cancer—one is still taking chemotherapy and one just finished radiation. I'll coordinate their schedules, but I want them rooming with you, Katie, since you have the most experience.

"Chelsea, I'm putting two girls in your room and, Lacey, you've got one to bed down each night. The main thing we want to do is work in tandem, do things as a group. The girls range in age from eleven to fourteen and I've got short bios on each one."

Kimbra passed around sheets of paper describing each new girl. Chelsea read the pages twice. She sure didn't want to mess up.

"I know you have questions, and we've got three planning sessions between now and tomorrow noon when they start arriving. Just remember, we're all in this together and the goal is to give each attendee the best summer experience possible."

"We'll do our best," Katie told Kimbra.

"Richard—Mr. Holloway said the three of you were especially close. That's why I wanted to be your supervisor." She smiled at the surprised expressions her statement caused. "You see, I know what it is to be a forever friend," Kimbra added. "And I know Jenny Crawford would have wanted you to stick together. So, come on—let's get started—tomorrow will be here before we know it."

Five

KATIE HAD LITTLE time to ponder Kimbra's remark about Jenny Crawford. There was too much she was expected to learn. Yet, Kimbra seemed to know more about the mysterious Jenny than anyone except Mr. Holloway, and because of the generosity of the One Last Wish Foundation toward her, Katie *always* wanted to learn more about her benefactor.

When she brought it up to Lacey and Chelsea that night before bed, Chelsea yawned and shrugged, and Lacey said, "What does it matter what Kimbra knows? Jenny's been dead for years. I'm worrying about getting these new girls situated." But still, Katie burned with curiosity.

At noon the next day, the kids began to arrive and by three o'clock the lobby of Jenny House was sheer bedlam. Katie held up signs with the names of her girls and one by one they came to her. Suzanne was a pretty twelve-year-old with a long mop of blond curls and puffy-looking face and hands. Latika was eleven, dark-eyed and tiny, and Dullas was thirteen, bald from cancer treatments and making no effort to hide it. Katie noticed that Dullas wore a constant sullen, disinterested expression, but she led them upstairs cheerfully, chattering to put the three newcomers at ease. "I'm Katie, and for this summer I'll be your Big Sister. If you need anything, come see me."

"I want that bed," Dullas announced the moment they were in the room. She pointed to the bed by the window.

Katie glanced at her file folder. "Suzanne's been assigned that bed."

"Well, unassign her," Dullas said, tossing her gear onto the bed. "It's mine."

Momentarily at a loss for words, Katie stared at the belligerent girl.

"I don't mind changing with her," Suzanne said meekly.

Katie didn't want to cause a scene, but she didn't want Dullas to think she could push everyone around either. Latika started to cry softly. Katie hurried to her side. "What's wrong?"

"I want to go home."

The training had prepared her for handling homesickness. "I'd like for you to stay, but I'll make a deal with you. How about trying it for a few days and then if you still want to leave, we'll go talk to Kimbra, who's our Bigger Sister. You'll meet her down in the rec room at four. We're going to have a party."

Katie leaned closer. "And this is *some* rec room too. I'd love to show it to you. Won't you give us a chance before you decide to leave?"

Latika wiped her hand across her eyes and sniffed.

"If the crybaby wants to go home, let her," Dullas announced, flopping onto her bed.

"We don't need that kind of talk," Katie told her.

"You'd better be nice to me," Dullas declared. "I have cancer."

Katie tapped the file folder. "*All* of you have cancer. It's no excuse to hurt someone's feelings."

Dullas shrugged indifferently. "So shoot me."

Katie ignored the surly girl and concentrated on helping Suzanne and Latika settle into the room. Dullas lay back on her duffel bag, pulled a baseball cap over her face, and ignored them until Katie insisted it was time for the party.

"Don't rush me," Dullas snapped when Katie asked her to hurry up.

In the hall, Katie ran into Lacey and her charge, Michelle, a frail twelve-year-old with cystic fibrosis. Together, they waited for the elevator, Dullas complaining mightily about its slowness. She uttered a swear word, shocking them all, and marched off toward the stairwell. "I'm walking down," she declared, in a tone that defied them to stop her.

"Don't trip," Lacey muttered under her breath loud enough for Katie to hear as the stairwell door clanged shut behind Dullas. Lacey added, "How'd you end up with Attila the Hun?"

"Lacey, that's not nice," Katie hissed, suppressing a smile. The other girls giggled. "I recall someone from last summer who had an 'attitude,' " Katie said. "We didn't send *her* home."

Lacey disregarded the comment and patted Michelle's shoulders. "Well, I have a real doll in my room."

The girl smiled shyly. "I'm glad I got to come. Because of my CF, I never get to go away. This is my first time ever."

Once down in the rec room, Katie searched for Chelsea. The room was crowded and kids were clustered around the video game machines. The giant-screen TV room was packed also. And a line had formed to play the Virtual Reality game, which is where Katie found Chelsea and her charges. Katie asked, "How's it going?"

"Terrific." Chelsea's eyes sparkled. "I love being here and helping out. I wish I could live here year round. But if you go off to college, this will probably be your last year, won't it?"

For days, Katie had been too occupied to think about her dilemma, but Chelsea's question brought it back with a jolt. "Probably so," Katie said. "But you and Lacey are supposed to carry on."

Katie led Suzanne and Latika toward the buffet table and saw Josh weaving through the crowd with a trio of young boys behind him. "Here she is," he called to the boys as he came up to Katie. "See— didn't I tell you to look for the prettiest girl in the room?"

The kids nodded agreeably and Josh grinned. Katie felt flustered. She introduced Suzanne and Latika and watched as they scampered off with the boys to play Virtual Reality. "How's it going?" Josh asked.

"Fine."

"We—um—haven't had much time together these past couple of days."

"We've both been busy."

"Are you still mad at me?" Josh peeked at her shyly as he asked.

"I'm not mad. I told you, I need time to think things out."

"I've come to a major decision. I've decided not to pester you. I've decided to keep my mouth shut and look so lonesome and forlorn that you'll take pity on me and go to college in Ann Arbor."

His expression looked so adorable that Katie couldn't stop herself from smiling. This was the Josh she knew and loved—sweet and caring. "I think that's a great decision." She felt a wave of relief. "I hate fighting with you, Josh. You mean too much to me."

His face split into a grin. "See! It's working already. You like me."

She patted his head. "Down, boy."

From the corner of her eye, Katie saw Dullas sidle up to the food table. Dullas stuffed a handful of potato chips into her mouth, then shoved another handful in the pockets of her shorts. Dumbfounded, Katie watched as Dullas made her way down the length of the table, systematically filling her pockets with food. She was so preoccupied with her task that she didn't see Katie until she was right up against her. "They feed us regularly," Katie said, crossing her arms and staring down at Dullas.

Dullas shot Katie a hateful look. "You have no right to spy on me."

"I wasn't spying. Your pockets resemble a chipmunk in autumn. You don't have to squirrel food away—there's plenty to go around."

"Drop dead."

"Hey, watch your mouth, kid," Josh interjected. "Katie's my girl and you can't talk to her like that."

"Your girlfriend?" Dullas measured him with a defiant glance. "You sure must be hard up." She spun around, pushed a kid out of her way, and got lost in the crowd.

"Who was *that?*" Josh asked. "And what's her problem?"

Katie shook her head. "I don't know what her problem is, but it's going to be a long summer if she doesn't come around."

"I can't believe they let her come to Jenny House if she's only going to stir up trouble."

"I'm giving her the benefit of the doubt—maybe she's scared and this is the way she hides it."

"Some act," Josh said. "She could win an Academy Award."

"Be kind."

Josh grinned, bent forward, and kissed the tip of Katie's nose. "I've got to go. I'm on kitchen duty. See you at dinner?"

Katie glanced toward Dullas's wake. "Maybe my little scavenger has taken enough food for our room to dine in tonight." Then she smiled playfully. "Go peel some potatoes."

She watched him move away and felt her spirits buoy. It felt good to be able to joke again with Josh. To have the tension that had been so taut between them dissolve. At least temporarily. Jenny House was a wonderful, magical place to Katie's way of thinking. For the first time in weeks, she was looking forward to her job. In spite of disagreeable Dullas.

Into every life, a little rain must fall. She reminded herself of one of her mother's favorite sayings. So let Dullas act nasty. Katie was determined to win her over. With effort, she was positive she could do it. Dullas was only thirteen years old and in treatment for cancer. How difficult could it be to soften her up?

Confidently, Katie went off to find her girls.

Six

⟨decorative flourish⟩

"If we don't slip off this afternoon while the kids are watching a movie, we may not get the chance again," Lacey told Katie and Chelsea. "Come on. Last one to the stables is a toad." Lacey took off running. Katie quickly caught up with her.

Chelsea was dreading arriving at the stables. They'd talked about riding up to the memorial for days, but hadn't gotten the opportunity. Now there was no more putting it off. Chelsea forced herself to go and arrived to see DJ leading two mounts out of their stalls.

"You need a horse too?" he asked Chelsea.

"Yes. A horse that's real tame. I'm not a very good rider."

"None of these horses is hard to ride," he said

without looking at her. "They're all tame as puppies."

Chelsea felt her neck redden. He must think her an awful wimp. Jillian had been a wonderful rider and Chelsea bet that DJ's Texas girlfriend, Shelby, could ride like a pro.

"I like to ride," she amended quickly. "It's only that I've never had much opportunity."

He led another horse out of its stall. "Do you want me to saddle her up for you?"

"That would be nice." Chelsea knew she could never have wrestled the heavy gear onto the horse's back. Especially with DJ watching. His expert fingers tightened the cinch under the horse's belly. She longed to talk to him, but he didn't seem interested in any conversation with her.

"Do you need a leg up?" he asked once the horse was ready to be mounted.

She did, but lied. "I can manage." She "managed" by not planting her foot firmly in the stirrup, and when she was partway up, her foot slipped, causing her to grab for the saddle horn. She found herself sprawled over the saddle like a sack of flour. The horse turned its head and looked at her with calm, patient brown eyes, making her feel even more foolish.

"Maybe you should start over," DJ said, tugging her off the saddle and setting her onto the ground. His hands felt warm and solid encircling her waist.

Mustering what dignity she could, Chelsea said, "Thanks."

This time, DJ held the stirrup steady with one

hand and gave her a boost with his other. When she was firmly seated atop the horse, he handed her the reins. "If you get into trouble, just give your horse her head—that means let her go—and she'll find her way home."

"I won't get into trouble," Chelsea said, feeling so embarrassed that her face burned. She urged the horse toward the trail where Katie and Lacey had already disappeared into the leafy glade. But the horse looked to DJ, as if waiting for his permission before taking off with a rider as green and un-schooled as Chelsea.

"Go on, girl." He clucked softly and slapped the horse's round rump. It obeyed by breaking into a trot, and Chelsea felt her fanny bouncing against the hard saddle. She could only imagine how undigni-fied she must look from the rear.

"What took you so long?" Lacey asked when Chel-sea finally drew alongside her and Katie. "Were you flirting with the stable help?"

"Just hush up, Lacey."

"Don't be so testy. I told you, if you like the guy, then go after him."

"Stop badgering me!"

"Hey, will you two knock it off," Katie said. "I don't want to listen to it. This is supposed to be a trip of respect. Not of sniping at each other. If I wanted sniping, I could have stayed at Jenny House and hung around Dullas."

"Sorry," Chelsea mumbled, feeling contrite.

"Me too," Lacey replied. "Speaking of Mary Pop-pins, what are you going to do about her? If we're going to begin work on the play we talked about doing, is she going to cooperate?"

"She and Suzanne go for chemo treatments this afternoon, and according to Kimbra, that may take some of the fight out of her. Kimbra said that her kind of chemo can make her sick."

Chelsea immediately felt sorry for Dullas, for she remembered what the nausea from medications felt like. She shuddered. "Is there anything we can do to help?" she asked.

"Stay out of her way," Lacey mumbled, not too kindly.

Katie ignored her barb. "I asked Kimbra what she knew about Dullas and she said that her situation's pretty bad. She's been living in Tampa, Florida, with a foster family. Her mother's gone and her father's in prison. When she got leukemia, her foster family couldn't take care of her anymore, so she was sent to Jenny House for the summer because Florida's HRS department didn't know what else to do with her. They're looking for a new home for her for when she comes back."

"What will happen to her if they don't find a place for her?" Chelsea was moved to pity by the facts.

Katie shrugged. "I don't know."

"No wonder she's the way she is," Chelsea added. "She's not had many breaks."

"It's still no excuse for her acting so bratty," Lacey interjected.

"But it helps us to understand her a little bit more," Chelsea said stubbornly. Lacey could be so maddening sometimes.

"She's lucky there's a place like Jenny House that she can come to," Katie said. "But it's only a temporary fix for her situation. I know she can act hateful, but I *do* feel sorry for her."

By now, the three riders had reached a place in the trail where they had to ride single file up the sloping side of the mountainous terrain leading to the flat plateau where they'd built their memorial to Amanda.

Chelsea kept remembering how ill she'd felt the last time they'd ridden up the trail. Her poor heart had been so weak and flabby that she'd scarcely been able to breathe. It had been in November, before her transplant, and Jillian had been with them. Chelsea filled her lungs with the sweet scent of the summer air and thanked God for the new heart beating inside her chest.

At the crest of the mountain, they dismounted, tied their horses to trees, and went the rest of the way on foot. Once on the flat rock of the plateau, the three of them fanned out to search for the tepee of twigs Lacey had tied together to form the memorial.

"Over here!" Katie called. "I found it."

Chelsea and Lacey hurried to where Katie was crouched, digging through a pile of dead leaves. The tepee was partially buried, and Chelsea held her breath, hoping that the laminated photo and Jillian's diamond stud earring were still tied to it.

"It's come apart," Katie said, lifting up the twigs in three parts. But from the corner of one of the sticks, the laminated photo dangled, and from its center the diamond caught the afternoon sunlight.

Lacey and Chelsea sent up a cheer. Lacey said, "Some animal's been nibbling on the corner of the photo—see?"

She held it up and Chelsea saw teeth marks. "I guess it didn't have much of an appetite for plastic," she said.

The photo looked faded, but Amanda still smiled from the center of their group. Chelsea felt a lump form in her throat. These days, she and Katie and Lacey looked older, more mature, healthier too. But Amanda looked the same, her gamine smile frozen in time. And ageless.

Lacey cleared her throat and said roughly, "What was I thinking—wearing my hair that way? Why didn't you two tell me how dorky I looked?"

"And me without any makeup," Chelsea added. "I guess I was too sick to care about such things."

Katie took the photo from Lacey's trembling fingers. "Yeah, we were quite a bunch, weren't we?"

"Well, we've got work to do." Lacey dusted her palms together and set about reattaching the tepee to the strips of leather that had come untied.

Katie gently removed the diamond and buffed it on the front of her T-shirt. "Just like new," she said, allowing the sun to glimmer off its surface. She reattached it to the photo, to a spot above Amanda's head.

In minutes, they had re-created the small memorial and planted it firmly into the ground. "I have an idea," Lacey said, then set about gathering small rocks and piling them around the base of each stick.

"Maybe this will keep it standing longer and keep little nibblers away."

When they were finished, they stood in a semicircle solemnly staring down at the marker. Chelsea missed her friends so much. It wasn't fair that Amanda and Jillian had died so young.

"We need to go." Katie took her hand and pulled her from the darkness of her thoughts.

Yet they hadn't taken but a few steps when Chelsea stopped, turned back toward the memorial, and felt a shiver of foreboding course through her.

"You all right?" Katie asked.

"I—I had a chill."

"But it's almost eighty degrees," Lacey said. "How can you be cold?"

"Not that kind of chill," Chelsea said. "Another kind. Like a premonition or something."

Katie and Lacey exchanged glances. "What about?"

"Like something bad is going to happen."

All around them, the air was thick with silence. Birds had stopped chirping and insects humming. "It's just the moment," Lacey said briskly. "It's just because we were all thinking so hard about Amanda and Jillian. That's all."

But Chelsea knew what she'd felt. And she'd always had an uncanny sixth sense. "No," she said. "It's more than that. Something bad is going to happen this summer. I know it is. I just know it."

Seven

"Do you LIKE the idea of writing and producing our own play?" Katie looked around the circle of girls seated in the rec room as she asked the question. They nodded enthusiastically. All except for Dullas, who sat slumped in her chair, her baseball cap pulled low over her eyes.

"We'd like one hundred percent participation," Lacey added, steadying her gaze on Dullas.

"It sounds like fun," Suzanne bubbled. Her thick curly hair bounced on her shoulders.

Chelsea offered, "And we'll be working with the boys from counselor McKensie's room, so we need to come up with a play that has plenty of parts for casting. We'll be making all the sets too, and Lacey will be in charge of makeup. And once the play's put together, it'll be videotaped for all of Jenny House to watch."

The younger girls giggled self-consciously and started discussing it among themselves. Katie asked, "Do you have any suggestions, Dullas?"

"I think it sounds stupid."

"And I think you need an attitude adjustment," Lacey quickly declared.

"Are *you* going to give it to me?"

Katie's hand shot out to keep Lacey from springing off her chair and possibly slugging Dullas. "Look, we'd like you to join in. This project is supposed to be fun."

"Well, *I'm* not having fun."

Ignoring Dullas, Chelsea picked up several notepads and passed them out. "Are any of you writers?" A few hands were raised.

"I have an idea." Suzanne spoke timidly. "Why don't we write a play about a bunch of sick kids who meet in a hospital and become friends and put on a talent show."

Several heads bobbed in approval. "And maybe their talent show can raise money for one kid's operation or something," Latika suggested.

Michelle had a sudden coughing spasm. Lacey scooted off her chair and knelt in front of the tiny girl plagued by cystic fibrosis. "Are you okay? Should I call one of the nurses?"

Michelle nodded to the first question and shook her head to the second. A fine sheen of perspiration had broken out on her face. "Please don't tell a nurse," Michelle whispered hoarsely between coughs. "They'll make me go to bed, and I want to work on the play more than anything."

"But if you're sick—"

"Please!" Michelle's eyes filled with tears.

Torn by indecision, Lacey looked to Katie, who shrugged. "All right," Lacey told Michelle. "But if you begin to feel worse, promise me you'll go straight up to bed."

Michelle promised, and the girls broke into small groups, with Chelsea taking charge of the writing session. Dullas remained slouched in her chair, refusing to join in the activity.

"What are we going to do with her?" Lacey asked Katie privately.

"I don't know. I've tried everything. In the room, she's a perfect slob, refusing to hang up any of her clothes or even to be polite to anyone. She hogs the bathroom and uses awful language. The others girls just ignore her, but I feel it's my responsibility to pull her into the Jenny House family, if you know what I mean. I'm a counselor, after all. I shouldn't let her get to me. She's just a kid."

Lacey nodded. "I know where you're coming from, but you can't *make* her have a good time. She's got to want to have fun."

"It's not as if we can send her home either. Kimbra says she still doesn't have a foster family lined up to take her. I feel sorry for her."

Lacey gave an impatient wave. "Pooh. I don't feel sorry for her. She has a choice, you know. She *can* make an effort." Lacey turned her attention back onto Katie. "How're things with you and Josh?"

"Peaceful coexistence right now. He hasn't bugged me once about college and the track scholarship offer. It's great to not have that tension between us— more like old times."

"But it won't last forever. Sooner or later you're going to have to make a choice."

"Later is fine with me," Katie said with a laugh.

Just then a shriek pierced the air and Katie and Lacey rushed toward the group of girls, who all sat gaping at Suzanne. Behind her stood Dullas. She was holding Suzanne's beautiful blond hair in her hand and smiling gleefully. "It's a *wig*," Dullas cried. "I *knew* your hair was fake and this proves it."

Suzanne sat sobbing, hiding her face with her hands. Her head was marked up with bright blue lines in a systematic pattern that indicated some form of medical technology.

Katie knelt to soothe and comfort her. The other girls looked horror-struck and Michelle began to weep empathetically.

Chelsea snatched the wig from Dullas and handed it to Katie. "It happened so fast," she said, sounding flustered. "I didn't even see her come up behind us."

"Why did you do it?" Katie demanded of Dullas, unable to hide the quiver of anger in her voice.

"She makes such a big deal of her hair every day. I figured she was trying to fool everybody into thinking it was really hers. She's just a big fake!"

Katie hugged Suzanne and placed the wig in the girl's lap. "It's all right, honey. You're beautiful with or without your wig, and you wear it if you want."

"What are the lines on your head for?" Latika asked, her eyes wide as saucers.

"I have some cancer in my brain," Suzanne said in a thick small voice. "The marks are so that the radiologist knows where to aim the X-ray machine to kill the bad cells. All my hair fell out. My daddy bought me the wig to wear until my hair grows back."

Katie stroked the luxurious blond hair and counted to ten under her breath. She had to deal with Dullas, yet all she felt like doing was slapping the girl. "Dullas, what you did was mean, and you owe Suzanne an apology."

Dullas blew air through her lips. "Fat chance."

Lacey stepped forward. "Allow me to handle this." She gripped Dullas firmly by the shoulders and marched her to the stairwell, opened the door, and pushed her inside. The door slammed shut with a metallic click that sounded like a shot. "Let's talk," Lacey said, her voice cold as ice in the hollow stairwell.

"Let go of me." Dullas twisted, trying to free herself.

"In due time." Lacey dug her fingers into Dullas's thin shoulders and glared down at the defiant girl. Dullas was a sloppy sight. Boxer shorts showed below the hem of each leg of her baggy shorts. Her T-shirt was stained and tattered on one arm. Her baseball cap was pulled low, hiding her eyes. Lacey pulled off the cap.

"Hey, give it back to me." Dullas made a grab, but Lacey held it out of her reach. Dullas's bald head looked pale and slick, and Lacey almost gave in to pity.

Lacey said, "I'll give it back to you once we get a few things straight. First of all, *I* don't feel sorry for you because you have cancer. I think you're a snotty little brat. But because you're in Katie's room and because Katie's my friend, I'm going to offer you some friendly advice."

Lacey leaned her face into Dullas's until their noses were almost touching. "Shape up and be nice or I'll personally make certain you have the most miserable summer of your earthly existence."

Dullas opened her mouth, but Lacey clamped her hand over it. "I'm not finished. Don't take me on, kid, because you'll lose. I'm bigger than you and a whole lot meaner. I know all the tricks because I've used them myself. In short, you've met your match, Dullas. Now, you march your little fanny out there, tell Suzanne you're sorry, and then start helping us with the play."

Lacey felt Dullas's mouth working against the palm of her hand. "Don't even think about biting me," she warned softly. "Because I will bite you back." She removed her hand.

Dullas glowered up at her. "I'll tell on you."

"And who are people going to believe?" Lacey put on her most innocent expression. "A valued counselor such as myself? Or a notorious brat?"

"I hate you!"

"You're breaking my heart."

"I never wanted to come here. HRS made me."

"Well, you *are* here, so make the best of it." Lacey

saw that Dullas was starting to look desperate, like a caged animal trapped in a corner. "There *are* worse places to be," Lacey ventured.

"How would you know?"

"I was in the hospital last spring," Lacey told her, surprising herself with her admission. "I hated the hospital, so most any place looks better to me than that. Especially a place like this where there's a hundred fun things to do."

"Everybody here is a fake. They say they care, but they don't. Nobody cares for nobody except themselves."

"I think you're wrong. I think everybody here cares, but you've got to be willing to let them care. You can't poke people with sticks and then wonder why they don't come around you."

"What do you know?"

"I told you, I wrote the book on how to alienate people with a single glance." She thought of Jeff. "And sometimes it's hard to convince people you've changed after you decide you want to belong again."

"Well, I'm not interested in changing. Or belonging. I just want all of you to leave me alone."

"That can be arranged," Lacey said. She stepped away from Dullas and reached for the door handle. "But if you want to be left alone, then we expect the same courtesy. *You* leave *us* alone too. No more mean pranks. No more ugly moods. Just crawl away and sulk all by your lonesome."

Confusion crossed Dullas's face. "That's what I want."

"A deal," Lacey said, holding out her hand. "Shake on it."

Tentatively, Dullas offered Lacey her hand. Lacey shook it firmly, turned, and marched out of the stairwell, leaving Dullas behind.

Yet the moment Lacey stepped into the rec room, she knew something was wrong. "It's Michelle," Katie told her. "We had to call a nurse. They've taken her to the infirmary. She's running a fever, Lacey. She's really sick. I'm sure they're going to send her home."

Eight

~

LACEY MISSED DINNER because she spent the evening sitting in the infirmary holding Michelle's hand. The girl was hooked to an oxygen tank and medicated, but she clung to Lacey fiercely. Lacey was told that Michelle's parents had been called and had given instructions for her to be transported to the nearest hospital where they would meet her and take her home. Lacey felt pity for Michelle and seethed silently. It wasn't fair that Michelle wanted to stay so much and couldn't. And Dullas wanted so much to leave and had to stay.

"There's always next year," Lacey told Michelle as an ambulance crew loaded her into the ambulance for the ride to the hospital. It was nearly dusk, and a small crowd of personnel had gathered to watch the departure. Kimbra tucked a teddy bear under the covers and assured Michelle that there would always be room for her at Jenny House. Lacey watched as the emergency vehicle pulled away, its lights making eerie crimson patches on the surrounding trees.

"You all right?" Kimbra asked.

"Fine," Lacey lied.

"We've still got the Western party going on down in the rec room tonight. You should come join us. It'll take your mind off Michelle."

"Thanks, but I'm not much in the mood."

Kimbra reached out and brushed Lacey's shoulder. "I'm really sorry. We'll do some juggling and get another camper for your room."

"No rush," Lacey said.

Once the others had left, Lacey headed toward the woods. The evening air felt cool and slightly damp. Thunder rumbled in the distant mountains, promising rain for later that night. In the quiet of the tree-draped trail, she finally allowed herself to cry, and she might have kept on crying if she hadn't heard Jeff calling her name. Quickly she wiped her eyes and answered. She saw him jogging toward her through the gloom and waited until he stopped in front of her.

"I've been looking for you," he said.

"I was just trying to get myself back together. I'm fine now."

"Are you?"

"I said I was, didn't I?" She turned, but he caught her and forced her to look into his eyes.

"Don't brush me off, Lacey. I know you're upset."

"Of course I'm upset. Wouldn't you be if the person you were in charge of got sick and had to go home?"

"It's a place for sick kids, Lacey. You should have figured something like this could happen."

"Well, I didn't." She crossed her arms defiantly. "And what are you going to do about it?"

"There's nothing I can do. Kimbra said she'll assign another girl to me. Easy come—easy go."

"Why do you act this way?"

"What way?"

"Why do you act like you're coping when you're not? Why don't you just admit that you hate being around sick people? That nothing's changed since last summer?"

She shoved him hard, almost throwing him off balance. "Don't go telling me how I feel! You don't know what I'm feeling or thinking."

Jeff quickly regained his balance and stepped in front of her again. "I know *exactly* what you're thinking and feeling. You're remembering last summer when Amanda got sick and died. You're scared that's going to happen to Michelle, aren't you?"

"Stop grilling me! I came to Jenny House to help and now I can't even do that."

"And what happened to Amanda never crossed your mind," he challenged.

"Of course it did." She was shouting at him, but couldn't stop herself. "And I've thought about how I almost died last spring. And how Katie almost died. And Chelsea. And let's not forget Jillian. She died just like Amanda. Don't tell me I don't know the facts of life at Jenny House, Jeff. I know them, all right. But you have no right to accuse me of pretending to ignore reality.

"I had a bad day, all right? Dullas acted like a perfect creep and I wanted to strangle her. Then Michelle got sick and had to be taken away by ambulance. Wouldn't that count as a bad day in anybody's book?"

"But you said you were fine when I asked you how you felt." His voice was low and almost growling. "Why didn't you tell me the truth the first time I asked?"

"Why should I?"

"Because I—" He stopped himself. "Because that's the way you handled things last summer and in Miami while you let your diabetes get out of control. You pretended all was well when it wasn't. And you pushed me away every chance you got."

Suddenly, it dawned on her what was bothering him. "Is that what you think I was doing? Pushing you away?"

"It's an old habit."

"Why should I push you away when we're such . . . good friends?" She let sarcasm drip over the words. "Am I still on trial, Jeff? Are you waiting for me to prove myself before you get close to me? Do you expect me to take a hike if you have a bleeding episode?"

Despite the dim light, she saw by the expression on his face that she'd hit the mark. "I don't have any expectations from you, Lacey."

"Liar."

The word hung in the air like a lead weight. From

far away, thunder rumbled and a cool breeze fluttered the branches of the overhead trees. Lacey caught the scent of rain dancing in the wind. It made her feel reckless and wild. "You *want* me to disappoint you. You want me to prove that you were right about me all along: 'Lacey can't change. She can't possibly care about some guy who's sick.' "

"You sent me that message often enough." Jeff sounded equally angry. "You dumped me for that Todd jerk and then expected me to fall at your feet after you had a change of heart in the hospital."

Lacey wondered how their conversation had gone from Michelle to Todd in only a few heated moments. "Is that what you think I did? Do you honestly believe I turned back to you because I had no one else?"

"Your timing was interesting. You wouldn't have anything to do with me until you got sick and Todd dropped you."

She rocked back on her heels, stunned by what she was hearing. "When I was sick, I reached out to you because I wanted *you* to be with me. But right now, I don't care what you believe about me. I see now that I can't change anything you believe because you're so determined to be right about me," she said coldly. "Well, you believe anything you want, Jeff McKensie, because I've *had* it with you. I'm tired of telling you I'm sorry about Todd and the way I ignored you. I'm finished apologizing. In fact," she added with a toss of her blond hair, "I'm finished with you, *period!*"

With that, Lacey spun on her heel and headed back toward Jenny House. She was all the way up on the deck when she realized that Jeff hadn't bothered to come after her. The realization squelched the last shred of hope for her and Jeff. Michelle was gone. Jeff was gone. There was nothing left for her at Jenny House. And therefore, no reason to stay for the remainder of the summer. Katie and Chelsea would be disappointed, but they'd have to accept her reasons.

In the lobby, she heard the strains of music and laughter coming from the rec room below. New tears pooled in her eyes. She felt left out. Alone. She caught sight of the giant portrait of Jenny Crawford and slowly walked to the stone fireplace where she allowed her gaze to linger over the beautiful ethereal face. Had Jenny ever felt lonely, she wondered?

"Lacey?" She heard Katie say her name from across the lobby. "Where've you been?"

"Walking," Lacey answered. "Thinking."

"About what?"

"About going home."

"But why?" Katie's large blue eyes reflected the lamplight. "Don't let Michelle's getting sick throw you. You're still needed here."

"Jeff and I had a huge fight," Lacey said tonelessly. "It's over between us, Katie. This time for good. It'll be too hard hanging around all summer seeing him and knowing we're through."

"But Jeff's not why you came," Katie reminded her. "You came to help."

"Help who?"

"We have the play and the video of it to make. We need you." Katie looked troubled. "Won't you please sleep on it? No need to make this kind of decision when you're bummed out. Things'll look better tomorrow."

"Katie—ever the optimist." Lacey managed a half-smile.

Latika yelled for Katie to hurry back to the party. "Coming," Katie returned. She backed away from Lacey, saying, "I've got to go, but please promise me you won't do anything until tomorrow. We'll talk again."

Lacey promised, but she knew her feelings wouldn't change by the morning. She felt like a failure and she wanted to go home. She rode the elevator up to her floor and stepped off. The halls were so quiet she felt like an intruder. With a sigh, Lacey went to her room, dreading going inside, knowing that Michelle's space was empty, her belongings packed up by some of the staff.

Lacey opened the room door and stopped cold in her tracks. There on Michelle's bed lay Dullas. Her baseball cap was pulled low over her eyes and she was flipping a basketball into the air and catching it. Her head rested on her duffel bag and more of her stuff was spread over the bed and nearby dresser.

"What are you doing here?" Lacey asked, shocked out of her numbness.

Dullas didn't bother to look at her as she answered. "I heard Michelle got shipped out, and so I figured you'd have room in here for me. I mean, I'm not nuts about being in Katie's room, so I thought I'd move in with you. You got a problem with that?"

Nine

❦

Lacey was absolutely speechless. She stared at Dullas as a hundred retorts ran through her head, but something, some instinct, warned her not to utter any of them. Instead, she asked, "How did you get in here? I locked the door."

"I picked the lock." Dullas sat upright on the bed and elevated the brim of her baseball cap. "But don't worry, I didn't steal any of your things."

Thoughts raced through Lacey's mind. Why had Dullas really come to her? How should she handle the situation? Did the disagreeable girl have a malicious motive? What would Katie do? If only she had more experience. To buy time, Lacey crossed to the desk positioned between the two beds and pulled out the chair. She sat down and studied Dullas coolly. "Answer me something, Dullas. This afternoon you told me you hated me. Now you want to move in bag and baggage. What gives?"

"I told you, I hate being in Katie's room."

"So in other words, you hate me less than you hate being in Katie's room. Is that the story?"

Dullas flashed Lacey a surly glare, but beneath it Lacey saw another, more subtle, emotion. *Fear of rejection?* "I don't expect you to like me the way you liked Michelle. But I hate being with those other girls, and so I figured with you being alone and all, I would tell you I was sorry for this afternoon and move into this room. But if you're going to get your nose out of joint—" Dullas crawled off the bed and tugged at her duffel bag.

"Hold up," Lacey said, making a quick decision. "I didn't say you couldn't stay."

Dullas eyed her suspiciously. "So I can stay?"

Lacey noted that Dullas hadn't asked, *"Can I stay?"* Why was she always so truculent? "I'll have to check with Kimbra."

"That's cool."

"And of course, if she agrees, I'll have a few rules for you."

"I should've figured there'd be strings."

Lacey ignored her whine. "First, clean up your act." Dullas mumbled an expletive. "Beginning with your language," Lacey demanded. "Second, I expect you to participate in our group's activities." Dullas groaned, but she didn't say anything crude. *Progress, of a sort,* Lacey told herself. "And third, change your attitude. We still have part of the summer ahead and I won't live with someone who hates every single minute she's here at Jenny House."

"I really don't like being here."

"Excuse me?" Lacey asked, leaning in closer. "I don't think I heard you correctly."

Dullas stared blankly, then caught on to Lacey's meaning. "Okay. Being here ain't so horrible."

"That's better." Lacey straightened. "Well, since we've missed most of the party, I think we should get ready for bed."

"Can I put my stuff away first?"

"Suits me." Lacey went into the bathroom and closed the door. She leaned heavily against the solid wood surface, her mind in a whirl. Minutes before, she'd been ready to pack up and go home. Yet Dullas's request to move in with her had changed her plans. She wasn't sure why she'd agreed. Agreeing meant staying at Jenny House.

Lacey shook her head, as if to clear out the muddle of emotions lodged there. So much had happened in the span of a few short hours, but the bottom line was that she had inherited Dullas, the most obnoxious female Lacey had ever met. "Why me?" she groaned under her breath. But, deep down, she knew why. She knew she wasn't a quitter. No matter what Jeff thought about her, Lacey Duval was no quitter.

"If you'd stick it out with her, we'd be grateful." Kimbra made her announcement to Lacey and Katie the next morning after breakfast in a small conference room in the administrative wing of Jenny House.

"I've been checking into sending her back to Tampa, but there's still no foster home for her yet."

"Small wonder," Lacey muttered.

"Look, I know Dullas is a problem kid, but she really has had a pretty rough life." Kimbra opened the folder in front of her. "Her mother split when she was eight. Her father was jailed for arson and insurance fraud when she was ten. Since she had no other relatives, she became a ward of the state and has lived in five foster homes in three years. Nine months ago she was diagnosed with leukemia. She underwent hospitalization and chemo, and the foster family that was keeping her just couldn't manage anymore. The state and federal government pay her medical bills, but what she really needs is a stable home environment."

"Poor kid," Katie said sympathetically. "No wonder she's so unfriendly. I guess it's hard for her to believe anybody honestly cares about her."

"She snores," Lacey grumbled, but the information about Dullas *did* affect her.

Kimbra tapped the tabletop thoughtfully. "You have a vote in this, Lacey. If you don't want to be responsible for Dullas, you don't have to be. But for some reason, she seems to have bonded with you. And if you're willing to give it a try, we'd be very appreciative."

Lacey glanced between the faces of Kimbra and Katie and saw that they were counting on her. She sighed. "I'm not heartless, you know. I'll make an effort with her."

A smile brightened Kimbra's face. "I'll tell Mr. Holloway. He'll be pleased. He told me you had a sweet streak regardless of how much you might try and hide it."

Lacey arched her eyebrow. "No reason to assassinate my character."

Kimbra laughed and stood. "You remind me a little of myself when I was your age. I had a similar frame of mind, but no matter how hard I tried to withdraw, I couldn't. Jenny always got me involved."

Katie bolted upright. "So you *did* know Jenny Crawford," she exclaimed. "Tell me about her. Please. I've wanted to know more for ages, but didn't know how to ask."

Kimbra appeared flustered. "That was years ago."

"Then what's the big secret?"

"No secret. It's nothing I talk about. Partly out of respect for her One Last Wish Foundation. Partly because even now, after almost twenty years, it's still painful to recall losing her."

"Please tell me," Katie pleaded.

"We met in the hospital. There were three other girls in our little group, but they all died. I was the only one to survive." She held up the stump of her arm. "And this reminds me of it every day."

"But what was Jenny like? How did she ever come up with the idea to give so much money away?" Katie asked. Lacey could tell that Katie was determined not to let Kimbra leave the room until her curiosity was satisfied.

Kimbra thought for a moment. "Actually, she had something in common with Dullas."

"Go on," Lacey chided.

"It's true. They were both parentless. Except that Jenny had a better break. She had a grandmother who took her in. I remember Mrs. Crawford vividly. Tough as a steel rod. Even resembled one. She was rich and powerful, and people quaked when she arched an eyebrow."

Lacey and Katie exchanged glances. "How did Jenny manage?" Katie wanted to know.

Kimbra smiled. "I've never known anyone so full of love and tenderness as Jenny. She melted that old woman's heart like fire melts ice. But that was Jenny's way. She simply loved you until you had to love her back."

"Did Mr. Holloway love her? I've seen him standing in the lobby staring up at her portrait."

"Boy, Katie, not much gets by you, does it?" Kimbra nodded. "Yes, he loved her. But he was older and her grandmother never approved of their relationship. Still, Jenny loved him with a passion. I remember when he'd come to see her in the hospital. Jenny's friends were green with envy. He was so handsome." Kimbra's smile faded. "He was with her when she died."

Lacey swallowed hard. The image of Mr. Holloway sitting by the bedside of the dying Jenny filled her mind's eye. "Sad," she said.

"Very sad," Kimbra agreed. "But between Jenny and her grandmother's generosity, we have Jenny House. And kids like Katie who didn't die. And people like me who got to grow up and have a career in nursing and counseling. I'm married and have two children, but when I heard that there was a need for volunteer staff for Jenny House, I gave up my summer to come and work here."

"You're a volunteer like we are?"

"Most of the staff are volunteers. As for me, I got to see Richard again. I got to see the results of Jenny's short life and death. It's worth it."

Once Kimbra had gone, Lacey and Katie sat looking at one another. "I had no idea," Katie said.

Lacey felt melancholy. In less than twenty-four hours, she'd lost Michelle and Jeff and gained Dullas. And she'd heard about a very unselfish and caring girl who did something wonderful with her life. Lacey longed to feel that same kind of altruism, but in truth, she dreaded spending the rest of the summer dealing with Dullas and not having Jeff as a boyfriend.

Katie pushed back her chair and stood. "Well, if memory serves, we've got a trail ride and a barbecue today. Maybe if we put Dullas between us, we can keep her under guard."

"Just the way I want to spend my day." Lacey sighed.

Katie looped her arm through Lacey's. "I'm proud of you, Lace. Deciding to take on dear Dullas. If anyone can bring her around, it's you."

Modestly hanging her head, Lacey drawled, "Aw, shucks. It's nothing."

She heard Katie laugh, but inwardly Lacey was anxious and unsure of herself. She knew that *she* was no Jenny Crawford.

Ten

⁓⸺⸺⸺⸺⸺

"WHY YOU DON'T ride up alongside DJ and start making small talk, Chelsea? If it were me, I would."

Lacey's advice only made Chelsea feel more self-conscious than ever. They were riding horseback through the woods toward a picnic site. All around them, kids were having fun, laughing and telling jokes from atop their horses. Even Dullas, who was sandwiched between Lacey and Katie, seemed to be enjoying herself. Chelsea glanced over at Lacey and said, "I'm telling you, he avoids me like I'm an untouchable or something."

"Lacey's right," Dullas piped in. "Nobody ever got nothing by doing nothing."

"Thank you," Lacey declared with a smug smile. "She has a point, you know."

Dullas seemed to visibly swell with pride over Lacey's praise.

"Guys fall at your feet," Chelsea told Lacey defensively. "You don't know what it's like to be rejected." Chelsea saw Lacey catch Katie's eye, but neither spoke. "Okay, you two, what are you hiding?"

"Lacey and Jeff are on the outs," Dullas offered. "I heard her talking to Katie about it."

"Eavesdropping is rude," Lacey insisted. "I thought you were going to behave yourself when you moved in with me."

"So sue me."

Ignoring the exchange between Dullas and Lacey, Chelsea asked, "Are you and Jeff having problems? Why didn't you say anything to me?"

"Jeff and I are finished," Lacey said matter-of-factly.

"No way."

Lacey waved away Chelsea's protest. "It's better this way. He'll never believe that I really care about him. He's expecting me to dump him, and nothing I say convinces him otherwise. So why disappoint him? I dumped him."

Chelsea wasn't fooled by Lacey's air of indifference. She started to press for further details, but Katie flashed her a signal to back off.

At that moment on the trail ride, the woods began to thin out and soon the group of riders was headed across a grassy field, toward picnic tables set up along a mountain stream. Eagerly, the horses pricked up their ears as they caught the sound of water. "I guess that's where we're headed," Chelsea said, feeling nervous over her horse's tug on the reins.

"Let's go faster," Dullas said as several of the riders spurred their horses into a trot across the field.

"You go on," Chelsea insisted to her friends. "I'll catch up." She saw DJ in the front of the group of riders. He rode tall, like a man accustomed to feeling the wind in his face. Still, he glanced quickly about, making sure that none of the riders got into trouble.

"Aw, come on," Dullas insisted.

"We'll get there," Lacey told her. "No need to rush."

"We'll stick with Chelsea," Katie said, holding her horse back from joining the others.

Behind her, Chelsea heard Dullas let out an exasperated grunt and knew Dullas wasn't pleased with the decision. "No guts," Dullas muttered loud enough for Chelsea to hear. "That's *your* problem, girl." Suddenly, without warning, Chelsea heard Dullas yell "Yah!" and heard her slap the rump of Chelsea's horse.

Chelsea screeched as her horse broke into a gallop. She dropped the reins and clung to the saddle horn for dear life, terror ripping through her. She felt herself slipping to one side of the saddle and watched the ground flying beneath the horse's pounding hooves.

Certain she could cling no longer, Chelsea shut her eyes, not wanting to see the hooves and ground strike her. Then, just as suddenly, she heard a rider alongside of her, felt a tugging at her horse's bridle. A voice said, "Whoa, fella. Whoa."

Miraculously, her horse slowed. When he finally halted, Chelsea slid to the ground in a heap. In a moment, her rescuer was off his horse and beside her. "Are you okay?" DJ asked.

Trembling, crying, Chelsea threw her arms around DJ. "I thought I was going to die," she sobbed.

"You really weren't going all that fast," he said. "But dropping the reins made it dangerous. If he'd stepped on them, he'd have gone down."

She clung to DJ and felt him stiffen. She struggled to regain her composure. "T-thank you for rescuing me."

A concerned group of counselors and friends soon surrounded them, all talking at once. "Is she all right?" Kimbra asked.

"I'm fine," Chelsea said weakly.

"Can you still ride?" DJ asked.

Her knees were shaking so badly, she was positive she couldn't get back up on the horse. "I'd rather walk," Chelsea told him.

DJ handed the reins of both his and Chelsea's horses up to one of the group. "I'll walk her to the tables," he said. "The horses are my responsibility. I should have been watching closer."

"It's not your fault," Lacey said with a grimace. "Let me deal with the problem that caused it." Chelsea watched Lacey ride off toward the stream where Dullas was lost somewhere in the crowd.

In minutes, the others had ridden away until only she and DJ were alone in the high grass of the field. Butterflies danced in front of them and the summer sun beat warm against Chelsea's head and shoulders.

Her heart slowed from its erratic pounding. "I'm sorry I'm such a bother," she said quietly. "I didn't mean to lose the reins. It all happened so fast."

"Just so long as you're okay."

Her heart turned a flip-flop. "I didn't think it mattered one way or the other to you if I fell off the face of the earth."

He looked down at her. "Why would you think that?"

"I know you don't like me very much." It took courage to tell him what she was thinking, but she figured her brush with death had made her extra brave.

"I guess it does seem that way to you, doesn't it?"

His answer surprised her for she'd expected him out of courtesy to brush aside her doubts. "I can't help what happened with Jillian."

He shook his head. "I don't hate you."

"What do you feel toward me?"

He didn't answer right away and she was afraid she'd pushed too hard. "I'm not sure," he told her at last. "You got the heart Jillian should have gotten. She was my twin sister. What can you expect me to feel?"

Chelsea knew DJ resented her, but what could she do?

"I would have traded places with her," Chelsea said. "I told Katie as much while we were waiting for the donor heart to arrive. I didn't want Jillian to die." She felt like crying.

"Look, I know it's not your fault. I know doctors and computers made the decision. They told us at the time that the donor organs could save three people this way instead of only one." DJ gave a bitter laugh. "Three for one. It sounds reasonable—except that the 'one' was *my* sister."

Chelsea understood his bitterness. There simply weren't enough donor organs to go around for all the people who needed them. She'd been lucky to get an organ in order to extend her life. Jillian, on the other hand, hadn't been so lucky. "More people should sign up to be donors," she said. "Both my parents have signed a place on their driver's licenses to be organ donors if they die in an accident or something."

"So have I," DJ said.

She glanced up quickly. "You have?"

"Why not? I won't need them if I'm dead. And I don't want some other brother going through what I've gone through."

"That's good of you. I—I'm glad to be alive. I always wished I knew who my donor was. Like Katie knows hers is Josh's brother. But I don't know. I'd like to tell the family thank you."

By now, they were almost at the picnic site. Chelsea understood why DJ didn't want to be around her. She was a constant reminder that she'd gotten the heart intended for Jillian. She didn't blame him, but it didn't stop her from feeling an overwhelming sense of sadness and loss. "Thank you again for rescuing me," she said.

"It's part of my job." Then he shrugged. "Besides, it would have been terrible if you'd survived heart transplant surgery and then died being thrown from a horse. A real waste."

He didn't add *of a good organ* but she sensed it was on his mind. She turned and walked quickly away, not wanting him to see the tears that were swimming in her eyes. All around her, kids were playing, eating, and laughing. Once more, she felt like a stranger looking through a window at a world she didn't belong to.

"Lacey said I had to apologize for making your horse run away with you."

Dullas's statement jerked Chelsea out of her gloomy mood. "You should be sorry," she snapped at Dullas. "You could have killed me."

The smaller girl offered a contrite if sullen glare. Her eyes were partially covered by the brim of the baseball cap and her clothes looked rumpled and dirty. "I didn't know you couldn't hang on to a horse." She cocked her head to one side, like a bird studying a worm. "But it wasn't all bad, you know."

"And just how do you figure that? What if DJ hadn't caught up with me?"

"That's just the point. He *did* catch you. And he walked you over here. And the two of you started talking. Isn't that what you wanted? Weren't you afraid to talk to him? Well, now you have. As I see it, I did you a favor."

Chelsea stared incredulously at Dullas. The girl flipped the brim of her baseball cap and skipped off. *Thank her?* Chelsea sputtered to herself. The girl was crazy. She wasn't thankful at all. At least for a while she'd held out some hope that DJ would notice her and care about her the way both she and Jillian had wanted him to care. Now she knew without a shadow of a doubt that DJ would never have anything to do with her. And now that her hope was gone, she felt more depressed than ever.

Eleven

Katie watched Chelsea wander off to be by herself and figured her talk with DJ must not have gone very well. Yet she refrained from hurrying over and pumping Chelsea for information. When Chelsea felt like discussing it, she would. Katie sighed, took a piece of watermelon off a table, and headed downstream.

The small creek bubbling over stones made a soothing, restful sound. She found a secluded place along its banks and sat down in the cool grass, bit into the succulent melon, and turned her thoughts to the letter she'd received that morning. Mail call had brought a message from the track coach at Arizona University wanting to know if she was intending to take the track scholarship he was offering. He'd written that time was running out and that there were others waiting for the scholarship if she didn't want it. Katie knew she wanted it, but she didn't have an answer.

She would have liked to talk it over with Josh, but, of course, Josh freaked out every time she so much as hinted at going away. And all of her friends were so bogged down in their own problems, she didn't feel she should burden them with hers. Truthfully, there wasn't anything they could say to her anyway. College and track and her desire to be on her own were out of their realm of understanding.

Jeff McKensie's voice interrupted her thoughts. "Can I join you?" He plopped on the grass next to her without waiting for her answer.

She put aside personal concerns and said, "This melon's great. Where's yours?"

"I'm not too hungry."

"Impossible. Last summer you ate everything that didn't eat you first." Last summer, they'd become good friends, often swimming laps in the pool together in the early morning.

"Last summer, life was simpler."

"How so?"

"I didn't realize how much grief there was in liking Lacey."

"You like her? According to her, you *don't* like her."

Jeff shook his head and sighed. "I like her. That's the problem."

"I'm confused," Katie admitted. "She thinks you don't like her. She said you had a big argument because you wouldn't believe that she cares about *you*."

"You bet I don't believe it. I wish you could have

seen her in the hospital last spring. She really screwed up her diabetes, Katie. When I saw her in ICU in diabetic coma, I felt sick to my stomach. She'd lost so much weight she looked like a war orphan. And all the while, she kept denying that anything was wrong with her. If she can't face reality, how can I trust her feelings toward me?"

Katie nodded with understanding. "I know how exasperating Lacey can be, but I think she knows where she went wrong with her illness. I think she's worked hard to be well again. What I don't understand is why you won't cut her any slack."

Jeff picked up a pebble and lobbed it into the gurgling brook. "Ever since last summer, I've been on a roller coaster with Lacey. First, she's interested in me. Then she's not. Do you know how many times she's given me the come-on, followed closely by the brush-off?"

Katie sensed his frustration, but she also felt obligated to defend her friend. "Don't you think the worst of it's over now? You might give her one more chance."

Jeff shook his head. "She's the one who announced that we're finished. I'm not putting myself on the line for her again."

"You provoked her. You know Lacey doesn't mean half of what she says when she gets mad."

"Exactly my point." Jeff leveled a green-eyed gaze straight at Katie. "I can't trust anything she says. Why should I believe her anymore?"

Katie felt a flush creep up her neck. In trying to plead Lacey's part, she'd helped Jeff be more convinced than ever that Lacey didn't mean what she'd said about caring for him. "Maybe you should be talking to Lacey about this stuff," she said.

"Can't you say something to her for me? You're the only person she's ever listened to."

"Give me a break, Jeff. I don't want to get in the middle of this. All I did last summer was run interference between you and Lacey and Amanda. I'm not up to it this year."

He looked hurt. "I need your help, Katie."

"I'm not Miss Fix-It, Jeff. I don't want to get involved. Really." She stood and brushed off the seat of her shorts. "I'm sorry if you're angry with me, but I'm staying out of your and Lacey's problems."

Katie hurried farther downstream where she could be alone. She felt bad about snapping at Jeff, but the truth was she couldn't even help herself, so how could she help him? Why didn't her friends understand that she had a life of her own and that she couldn't solve the world's troubles? "Good old Katie," she muttered under her breath. "Got a problem? Take it to Katie."

She heard a horse whinny and turned to see Josh riding toward her. "I've been looking for you," he said, dismounting in front of her.

"Good grief, can't I get any privacy?"

He stepped backward. "Sorry. Kimbra wanted all the counselors back at the picnic site for some games. I said I'd find you and let you know."

"I—I'm sorry," she stammered. "I didn't mean to be rude. I'll walk back with you."

"What's wrong, Katie?"

She saw concern and wariness in his eyes, but couldn't bring herself to mention the letter. She didn't need another confrontation with Josh at the moment. "Nothing much," she said. "Jeff was just dumping on me about his and Lacey's problems and I was feeling helpless."

Josh looked relieved. "Yeah, it's best to stay out of the path of those two. I don't think they're ever going to get it right between them." He put his arm around her shoulders and hugged her. "They're not like us, huh? We know we want to be with each other."

She fell into step beside him as he led the horse toward the picnic area. *Coward!* her mind accused. Why hadn't she told Josh the truth? More and more, she felt herself drifting farther away from him and her life in Ann Arbor. Every day she was filled with a restless yearning for something else. Something more. "Not like us at all . . ." she repeated, feeling as hollow and empty as an abandoned dream.

"I ache all over. How can anyone think that horseback riding is fun?" Chelsea moaned from her bed.

"Soak in a tub of warm water," Lacey suggested. She was in Katie and Chelsea's room playing with different hairstyles in front of the mirror.

"Where's your shadow?" Katie asked. "How'd you get away from Dullas?"

Lacey grimaced. "I insisted she play some video games with one of the guys from Josh's room. Honestly, she's driving me crazy with her hanging around."

"Don't be mean," Chelsea chided. "I think she's got a case of hero worship."

"Why should she?" Lacey asked. "I'm not particularly nice to her."

"So what's news about that?" Katie said innocently.

Holding up a hunk of her hair and a comb, Lacey turned from the mirror to face Chelsea and Katie. "Well, thank you, my good friends. Since when did you two decide to trash Lacey? Is this a new pastime? Are we bored?"

"Leave me out of this," Chelsea moaned. She got up from the bed. "I am going to soak in the tub." She disappeared into the bathroom.

"So what's with you?" Lacey asked, eyeing Katie.

Katie told her about the coach's letter and finished by saying, "I have to make a decision soon."

"You're going to have to tell Josh. He thinks you're going to *marry* him. He needs to know you're going off to Arizona."

"I didn't say that."

"It's what you want to do. Just do it."

Exasperation welled up in Katie. Lacey made it sound so simplistic. "What if I told you I've decided not to take the scholarship. That I'm going to college in Ann Arbor and marry Josh next spring."

"Then do that. Just *do* something, Katie."

Katie felt like exploding, but just then Dullas came bounding through the doorway. "Don't you know to knock?" Katie snapped.

"Why should I? Are you telling secrets?"

"Back off, Dullas," Lacey said. "Knocking is polite."

"I'll remember that for next time." Dullas held out a folded piece of paper to Katie. "Some guy asked me to give this to you."

"What guy?"

"Some guy in the lobby. I didn't ask for his family history."

Katie snatched the piece of paper and unfolded it. *Probably someone else wanting advice,* she thought sourly. She wished people would leave her alone. The note read: "Meet me on the hiking trail."

"Who's it from?" Lacey asked.

"There's no signature." She looked at Dullas. "Are you sure this isn't a trick?"

"Look, don't go. I don't care one way or the other. And who cares if the guy waits all night on the trail?" Dullas flopped on one of the beds and watched Lacey comb her long blond hair.

Suddenly, Katie wanted to go. She *had* to get out of the room before she screamed. "I'll go check it out." She headed for the door. "But if this is one of your pranks . . ."

Dullas shrugged. "Look, I thought I was doing you a favor."

Katie snatched up a sweater and hurried out of the room.

Twelve

The hiking trail was brightly lit by moonlight as Katie hurried to her rendezvous with the mysterious note sender. Curiosity tempered her anger, but she knew she'd personally throttle Dullas if this was a wild-goose chase. She rounded a bend in the trail and saw a male figure standing in the middle of the path. He was tall and was wearing a baseball cap. His hands were thrust into the pockets of a lightweight jacket.

"Hello," Katie called. "Who's there?"

"It's Garrison Reilly." She skidded to a halt in front of him, too amazed to say anything. Garrison grinned. "Surprise."

"But how—? I thought you were back in Ann Arbor."

"My dad's teaching a writer's conference at Duke

University all this week. I knew where you were and took a chance and drove over."

"Why didn't you call or write that you were coming?"

"I wasn't sure you'd see me if I asked ahead of time." He continued to grin down at her. "Haven't you heard? It's easier to ask forgiveness than to get permission."

She returned his smile and felt the old familiar rapid thudding of her heart that she often experienced when she was near him. She loved Josh, but there was no denying that Garrison made her pulse race. "I forgive you for surprising me," she said. "And if you'd asked, I'd have given you permission to come visit me."

"I didn't want to cause trouble between you and Josh either."

She sobered. He was right—Josh wouldn't be pleased if he knew she was standing in the moonlight with Garrison. "Josh is more mature than that," she said, feeling a need to defend Josh.

"Still, I thought it would be better this way. Now you can tell him, or not. Your choice."

She pushed that particular problem aside and asked, "Where are you staying?"

"I'll drive back to Duke tonight. It's only a couple of hours."

"I could have been busy tonight. You took a chance on coming to see me."

"It was worth it."

She felt her mouth go dry. Why did he have such

an effect on her? "It's good to see you," she confessed.

"Besides, I wasn't sure if you'd be home before I left for college."

"Where?"

"I got accepted at Princeton."

"Wow," Katie whispered, "I'm totally impressed. An Ivy League school like that is big time."

"What about you?"

"No place like Princeton."

"But you *did* get accepted to some place besides Michigan?"

She heard herself telling him about the scholarship offer to Arizona before she could stop herself. She told him everything—all her confused feelings about leaving home, about wanting to run track, about the resistance from friends and family.

"You mean Josh, don't you?" he asked. "*He's* the one who's really holding you back, isn't he?"

She dipped her head, ashamed to admit it to Garrison. "He isn't trying to be mean or anything. He just cares about me. About us."

Garrison took her hand. "Take a walk with me." Obediently, she went, enjoying the warmth of his hand on hers, his nearness. "You know, Katie, I liked you from the first time I laid eyes on you in English class."

"Even though I tried to ignore you?"

"Especially then." Moonlight lay on the scattered leaves in front of them on the trail. Katie shuffled through the dry foliage, sending the beams off into the shadows. Garrison said, "And when we worked on our paper together, I saw that you were smart. And when I watched you run at track meets, I saw that you were talented."

"You came to the track meets?"

"Most of them." Somehow, his admission delighted her. "Anyway," he continued, "the thing that impressed me most of all is how you kept on going in spite of your heart transplant. Do you know there are people who would have given up all thoughts of a regular life if they'd had to face a transplant?"

"I never wanted to give up my dreams because of my health," she told Garrison. "In fact, running track again is what helped me recover and recuperate faster."

"If that's the way you feel, then what you just told me about being undecided over taking that scholarship doesn't make any sense." He stopped walking and turned her by the shoulders and gazed down at her. "You know what you want, Katie. What's really holding you back?"

"I—I don't know what you want me to say."

"Is it Josh? Is he stopping you?"

"No."

She said the word too quickly, and Garrison dug his fingers into her shoulders. "Tell me the truth."

She didn't owe him any explanations, but she was desperate to talk out her feelings. "Josh is part of it," she admitted.

"What's the other part?"

Moonlight spilled over Garrison's broad shoulders and she felt the urge to touch it, as one might brush fingers across a glass top. Would the moonlight feel cool, like glass? Or warm from the heat of his body? "I'm scared," she whispered. "I'm scared of moving so far away from home and my doctors and everything that's safe."

Garrison nodded and gently pulled her against his chest. He stroked her hair and ran his fingers down the side of her cheek. "Who wouldn't be scared? It shows you have good sense."

She pulled away. "But why should I be? I've wanted this all my life. Once, I dreamed of running in the Olympics, and the first step on that road is a successful college running career."

"The Olympics?" He smiled and stroked her cheek with the back of his hand. "You *do* dream big, Katie O'Roark."

"I've pretty much given up that part. But the other —running track in college—is still something I want. But what if I get out there and something goes wrong with my heart? It's Josh's brother's heart inside me. And I feel I should do whatever's necessary to keep it safe."

Once the words were out, Katie realized that was honestly her deepest fear. Until then, she'd thought that she'd only been afraid for her own safety. "He lost his brother," she continued. "And if I die, in a sense he'll lose us both forever."

"We all have to die, Katie."

"I know that. But I got a second chance at life. Getting a transplant is an awesome responsibility. I can't be stupid about it. Or careless."

Garrison hooked his hands behind her waist and

gazed up through the canopy of moon-studded trees. "Josh's brother was an athlete, wasn't he?"

"A football player. He died on the field."

"If he's up there looking down at you," he gestured toward the starry sky, "don't you think he's pleased knowing another athlete got his heart?"

She followed Garrison's gaze upward. "I'd like to think so."

"And if that's the case, don't you think he'd want you to carry on with the athletic career he can never have?"

She'd never thought about it that way before. Never imagined what Aaron might have wanted. What dreams he never got to fulfill. "You ask hard questions, Garrison."

He returned his gaze to her upturned face. "My father always said I had the Gift of Questions." He chuckled. "Maybe I'll be a lawyer or something."

"You'd make a good one."

He stood there in the moonlight looking down at her face for the longest time. For a moment or two, she thought he might kiss her. She remembered when he'd kissed her at his Christmas party and trembled slightly. But he didn't kiss her. He unlocked his fingers from behind her waist and stepped backward. "You know, Katie, I'll be home next summer from college. If you and Josh can't work things out . . ." He let his sentence trail.

"You'll meet smart, beautiful girls at Princeton and forget my name."

He grinned. "We'll see." He jammed his hands

into his jacket pockets and she heard him rattle his car keys. "It's late, and I have a long drive."

"I thought you said it wasn't so long."

"It's long enough."

They headed back up the trail toward Jenny House. "I'm glad you came," she said when they neared the parking lot. "It was nice of you to come out of your way and surprise me."

"I just knew I wanted to see you again and I wasn't sure I'd be able to unless I drove up here." He looked over at the soaring structure that was Jenny House. The windows glowed brightly with lights and kids could be seen in the lobby and on the broad wooden deck. "Nice place," Garrison said.

"It's a wonderful place." Briefly, she told him about Jenny Crawford.

"So she managed to achieve her dream even though she died," Garrison mused.

"I don't think it was her dream until she got sick."

He tipped her chin with his finger. "You think about what we discussed before you go telling that coach 'no' to his scholarship offer. And you write me while I'm at Princeton. I'll leave my address with your parents."

Katie watched Garrison jog through the parking lot, get into his car, and drive away. She stood watching long after his car was gone, long after his tail-lights had disappeared into the night. A strange and wistful longing filled her. She raised her face upward, closed her eyes, and let the moonlight wash over her skin, like silken water. "So, Aaron," she asked quietly, "what do *you* think I should do?"

Thirteen

❧

"Is it me, or is Dullas actually trying harder to be a human being?" Katie asked the question after she, Lacey, and Chelsea had wrapped up the work on the play for the day.

Everyone had been given a free time and so the three friends had gone into the snack shop at Jenny House and ordered sodas, ice cream, and french fries. Lacey had carefully allotted herself a diet soda and a small portion of each food. "I think she's trying harder," Lacey said between bites. "Just this morning, she asked me if I could help her get a wig."

"And you said?"

"I told her I'd ask Kimbra."

"Gosh, Lacey," Katie declared with an impish grin, "you just might have a career as a social worker ahead of you."

"Very funny."

"She is doing better with you," Chelsea said. "You've got to admit that much."

"I admit nothing. I just don't put up with any of her meanness. It's a battle of the wills and mine's stronger than hers." Lacey sipped from her straw, set down her glass, and turned to Katie. "So, are we never going to hear who your mysterious visitor was last night?"

"No one special."

Lacey looked exasperated. "Don't you know there's a fine art to fibbing? Your fibs are written all over your face, Katie O'Roark. Like words on a book."

Katie felt herself blush.

"Maybe she doesn't want to say," Chelsea insisted. "She has a right to privacy, you know."

"Well, excuse me." Lacey looked miffed, but Katie appreciated Chelsea's stance. She honestly wasn't ready to talk about Garrison's visit. Mostly because the news would get back to Josh and she wanted to be the one to tell him.

All at once, Latika and Suzanne came running into the snack shop. "Come quick!" Suzanne cried. "Dullas has gone crazy and she's trashing your room."

Katie was the first out the door, followed closely by Lacey and Chelsea. The younger girls trailed behind. They bypassed the elevator and raced up the stairwell, where their footsteps made echoing, hollow sounds. When they reached the closed door of Lacey's room, they stopped. From the other side of the door, Katie heard the sounds of objects hitting the walls and muffled cries. "Maybe we'd better get a staffer," Katie said.

But Lacey stepped up to the door and grasped the knob. "Not yet. Let me see what's going on."

"It could be dangerous."

"Not much but clothes and books to throw," Lacey said. Yet her heart pounded anxiously.

"There're your makeup bottles," Chelsea said.

"I'll kill her," Lacey insisted. She pushed her friends away from the door. "Please, let me try calming her down first. If I scream for help, then go get somebody on staff."

"I don't know—"

"She *is* my responsibility," Lacey reminded Katie. Swallowing hard, Lacey pushed open the door and stepped inside the room.

It looked in shambles. Clothes were strewn everywhere. Drawers had been pulled to the floor and a bed pillow had been ripped. A flurry of feathers fluttered through the air. Dullas was down on her knees, busily tossing things out of the closet and sobbing. Lacey closed the door behind her and took a deep breath. "You'd better have a good explanation for this one, roomie."

Dullas stopped mid-sob and rose shakily to her feet. "Go away!"

"I live here, remember?" Lacey gripped the doorknob behind her back, both for support and for the possibility of needing a quick getaway. "If you wanted to rearrange the room, you might have checked with me first."

Dullas spun. Tears were streaming down her

cheeks and she looked terrible. "I—I—" Her voice broke. Suddenly, she ran to Lacey, threw her arms around her, and buried her face in Lacey's T-shirt.

Stunned by the unexpected move, Lacey stood motionless, then very slowly, she encircled the crying girl with her arms. Minutes passed. Finally, Lacey ran her hand over the top of Dullas's head in an attempt to soothe her. Dullas's skin felt smooth and tight, with the softest fringe of downy hair on the back of her skull. "Let's sit down and talk about it," Lacey said when Dullas's sobs tapered off.

Lacey led her to a bed and sat down with her, keeping her arm around her shoulders.

"You two all right?" Katie opened the door and stuck her head inside the room. "It got quiet all of a sudden."

"We're fine," Lacey told her, watching Katie's eyes grow large at the sight of the damage.

"Should I call for reinforcements?"

"No. Dullas and I are about to talk this out."

"If you need anything—"

"Everything's under control."

Katie shut the door and Dullas looked up at Lacey. "Are you going to have me kicked out?"

Lacey surveyed the wrecked room. She was upset, but realized there had to be an explanation. "My room at home looks like this, and that's just when I'm getting ready for a date." She felt amazed at her own ability to remain calm.

Dullas sniffed and Lacey found an overturned box of tissue on the floor and handed several to the girl. "It—it was the letter," Dullas said.

"What letter?"

Dullas rummaged around through the piles of clothes strewn over the bed and extracted a piece of paper. "It's from my dad."

Lacey took the paper. The top bore the letterhead of the state of Florida penal system. The handwriting looked scrawled and disjointed. Lacey squinted to make sense of it.

Dullas snatched it away. "He wrote to say he was denied parole and that it'll be another couple of years before his chance for one comes up again." She paused. "And that he thinks it's best to give me up for adoption." Dullas muffled a sob. "How do you like that? After three stinking years in foster homes, after thinking that one day he and I might have a home together, he decides to dump me. Just like my mom did."

Dismayed, Lacey offered, "Well, maybe it's for the best. I mean, now instead of foster homes, you can get a real home. Adoption isn't so bad. There's a girl at my school who's adopted—"

Dullas exploded. "Get off it! Don't you know anything? People only want cute little babies. No one wants an ugly thirteen-year-old. Especially a bald one with cancer."

Lacey had no snappy comeback this time. "I don't know what to tell you."

"Anyhow, HRS was going to stick me in another foster home. So I guess it doesn't matter anyway if he dumps me."

"It matters," Lacey said. "It mattered to me when

my parents split up last Christmas. But there wasn't anything I could do about it either."

"You still have a home though, don't you?"

"I live with my mom. Visit with Dad every other weekend or so."

"At least they *care* about you. About what happens to you."

Lacey had to admit that Dullas had a point. No matter how much her parents battled with each other, neither had made her think that she wasn't important. "Maybe your dad cares about what happens to you too. I mean, it doesn't seem like there's too much he can do for you if he's stuck in jail."

Dullas's lower lip trembled. "He doesn't have to throw me away. Like I was garbage."

Lacey winced at the pain she saw on Dullas's face. At the hurt she felt for the girl. "I wish I could make it better," she said. "But I can't."

"Are you mad at me? Are you going to make them send me away?"

"You said you hated it here."

"It's not so bad."

Lacey squeezed Dullas's thin shoulders tightly. "Welcome to the Jenny House family." She stood and studied the wrecked room. "You've got an hour before dinner. So let's start cleaning up."

"You'll help me?"

"Don't look so shocked." Lacey stooped and began to gather up clothing. "I've thrown a few temper tantrums myself, and my friends, Katie and Chelsea, stuck by me."

"Are you saying we're friends?"

"Well, we haven't made very good enemies, have we?"

Dullas shook her head. "I really have been trying harder, you know."

"I know," Lacey conceded. She hesitated. "We don't have to clean this up by ourselves, you know. Katie and the others will help if we ask."

"They hate me."

"Are you so sure?" Lacey crossed to the door and opened it. There in the hall, sitting cross-legged on the floor were Katie, Chelsea, Suzanne, and Latika. "You all busy?" she asked.

They scrambled to their feet and edged into the room. "Major earthquake," Suzanne said, looking around.

"Dullas and I need some help getting it back into shape before dinner. Any volunteers?" Lacey eyed each of the girls, all but daring any to refuse.

"I'll help," Chelsea said, picking up a drawer.

"Me too." Katie shuffled through a pile of shoes and started for the closet.

"Thanks," Dullas mumbled as everyone set to work.

"It's history," Lacey said breezily, knowing it wasn't easy for Dullas to be grateful to anybody. "And you did have the good sense not to smash my things."

Dullas gave her a tentative look and allowed the smallest bit of humor into her quavering voice as she said, "No way. Not even I'm *that* brave."

Fourteen

⁓

By the next morning, Dullas's actions were the talk of Jenny House. And Lacey found herself in Mr. Holloway's office in a meeting with him and Kimbra concerning Dullas. "Is she dangerous?" Kimbra asked. "We can't have someone staying who might harm others. Or herself, for that matter."

"No," Lacey told the two worried adults. "She's not dangerous. She got a letter from her dad and it upset her, so she reacted to it."

"More like overreacted," Richard Holloway said. "Look, Lacey, you don't have to stay in the same room with her. We can move her into one of the adults' rooms and keep her under surveillance. In fact, I'm thinking that perhaps we should go ahead and make arrangements for her to leave as soon as possible."

"Where would she go? Kimbra said HRS in Florida hasn't found another foster home for her."

"She'd be put into a group home until other arrangements could be made," Kimbra said.

"You mean a place where she lives with a bunch of other girls that nobody wants? Where they keep you under lock and key?"

"It isn't like a jail. It's just a temporary place. Until a more suitable home can be found for her."

"But what if she doesn't get another home?"

"Then she'd stay in the group house until she's of legal age."

"That's awful," Lacey cried. "What about the fact that she's got leukemia? Who'd take care of her?"

"She'd be under constant supervision. She'd go for regular medical checkups and attend school just like any other girl."

"But it's not like being in a *family*," Lacey said stubbornly. "She needs to be living with a family."

"A group home may be the best we can do." Kimbra looked concerned as she attempted to calm Lacey's fears.

Mr. Holloway interrupted. "As I said, maybe we should start looking for a suitable group environment for her now."

"I'm telling you, things are okay. She just trashed a room. We all pitched in and put it back into shape. It's good as new."

"That's not the point. We can't have someone act so violently just because they get some bad news."

"Bad news!" Lacey jumped to her feet. "An F on a math test is bad news. Dullas got told by her own father that he was giving her away. I'd say she got more than bad news."

"From what reports about him tell us, he wasn't much of a father," Kimbra said gently. "He was always in trouble with the police. He earned a living as an arsonist—for a price he'd set fires to enable other people to defraud insurance companies. He used to go off and leave Dullas alone in their apartment with no food and no phone. The state had to take her into protective custody for her own safety."

Lacey glanced between their two concerned expressions. "Kids don't get to pick their parents. But that doesn't mean you don't want to be part of a family. Dullas isn't any different than any of us in that way. Didn't you tell me that Jenny Crawford was an orphan?"

Kimbra nodded.

"Well, I'll bet that even though her grandmother loved her like crazy, Jenny still wanted to have her parents with her. Love, or no love, doesn't change what a person wants deep down in her heart."

Richard studied Lacey thoughtfully. "You're right, of course. My years as an attorney left me with an aptitude for judging human nature, so I hear what you're saying." He leaned back into his leather desk chair. "You're telling us that Dullas isn't a threat to anybody. She's wild and unpredictable, but not in a dangerous way."

"Exactly."

"And you want to ride out the remainder of the summer with her."

Lacey swallowed hard, realizing she was being

given even more responsibility, but she knew she didn't have a choice. She couldn't let them send Dullas away. "Yes. We only have five weeks before we all have to go home. Maybe by then, another foster family will be found to take Dullas."

"Maybe," Kimbra said.

Lacey started for the door and heard Richard say, "But if there's one more peep of trouble out of her, she's leaving."

"I think she's over the worst of it, Mr. Holloway. I really do. She's helping with our play and trying much harder to get along with the other kids."

Lacey escaped from Mr. Holloway's office and hurried to the lobby, where kids were working on the play. Dullas was seated at a table writing on a tablet while Chelsea was dictating. Dullas looked calm and concentrated, the picture of cooperation.

"How'd it go?" Katie whispered in Lacey's ear.

"They wanted to send her away, but I talked them out of it."

Katie looked surprised. "It was a legitimate way of getting rid of her. Why'd you do it?"

"I feel sorry for her."

"So did I. At first."

"Yeah, well, you know how I hate to have people telling me what to do."

"You're really a softie underneath, aren't you."

Lacey offered a frosty stare. "Why are you insulting me? I'm tough and mean. And don't forget it."

Katie smiled at her. "Never."

Lacey offered a sheepish smile in return. "This

growing up and acting like an adult is hard stuff, Katie."

"You got that right." Katie gazed wistfully at the younger girls giggling together as they worked and thought of herself before the days of her heart transplant. The days before surgery and antirejection medications when she ran without worrying and dreamed of the Olympics. "It's the hardest thing in the world."

"Katie, wait up," Josh called.

Katie was on her way down to the cafeteria for dinner with the gang. "Hi," she said, smiling. She'd been so busy the past couple of days that she'd hardly seen Josh at all. She told the others to go on without her. "What's up?"

"That's what I'm asking you."

By now, the lobby was empty and Josh had walked with her over to the stone fireplace. "What do you mean?"

"Someone said you met some guy out on the hiking trail a few nights ago," Josh blurted. "Is it true?"

Katie's good humor evaporated and her stomach tensed. "Who told you that?"

"It doesn't matter. Is it true?"

She saw anger in the challenging glare of his eyes. It had been weeks since they'd argued and she'd almost forgotten the awful tension she felt when he acted possessive. She returned his glare and realized with a start that she was sick and tired of continuously walking on eggshells around him. "If you must know, Garrison drove over to say hello from Duke, where his father was teaching a seminar."

"Garrison! I thought you and he were history."

"Stop it, Josh! Stop it, this minute." Katie felt her blood pounding in her ears. "He and I are friends and all we've ever been is friends. *You're* the one who keeps trying to read something into him and me."

"Yeah, he's your friend, all right. He made it clear that he wanted to date you."

"But I didn't date him, Josh. I've never dated any-body but you." She crossed her arms, every muscle in her body taut. "And maybe that's part of the whole problem. Maybe I should have dated him. Maybe I should be dating lots of other guys. Maybe dating others would help me figure out what I really feel toward you."

"What's that supposed to mean? That I'm not good enough for you?"

"No. That I'm not ready to settle down." She spun, but he caught her arm. She pulled it from his grasp. "And since we're at each other's throats, you may as well know that the Arizona coach wrote me about the scholarship again. He needs an answer about my intentions, or he's going to withdraw his offer."

Some of the angry red color drained from Josh's face. "Aren't you going to tell him you haven't made up your mind yet?"

"You'd like that, wouldn't you? You'd like me to keep riding the fence until the offer's withdrawn and I have no choice but to stay home in Michigan."

"That's not fair. You know I want to see you run track."

"Sure—so long as it's on your terms."

"But what about us, Katie? What about our plans? What about me wanting to marry you?"

She was shaking now, and tears were threatening to erupt. She forced them down, knowing she didn't want to cry like a baby. "Let me ask you something, Josh. What did your brother want to do with his life?"

"Aaron? What's he got to do with this?"

She balled her fist against her breast. "His heart's inside me and I'm responsible for it. And I want to know what he wanted for his life. What he dreamed about."

Katie saw moisture spring into Josh's blue eyes. "He wanted to play football. H-he used to wonder if he was good enough to be drafted by the NFL. He told me that if he had a good four years at Michigan, he'd be in the running for a pro career."

"Did you want that for him?"

"Yes."

"Then why can't you want it for *me*? Why can't you let me go after what *I* want?"

Silence hung over them in the lodge. If she lived to be a hundred, she'd never forget the expression of turmoil and pain on Josh's face. She hated herself for causing it. She felt a sick sensation in the pit of her stomach.

He didn't answer her. And then the glass double doors of the lobby swung open and DJ barreled into the lodge. He yelled, "Quick! Call an ambulance. Jeff's been kicked by a horse!"

Fifteen

❧

Katie paced the floor of the hospital waiting room while glancing anxiously at Lacey, who sat hunched over in a chair staring at the carpet. Had it only been last summer since they'd been in that very room waiting in shifts to visit Amanda? It seemed uncanny that the same people were waiting once more for news about a member of Jenny House: herself, Lacey, and Chelsea. Missing was Jeff. This time *he* was the patient, and he was still down in the emergency room. At least Mr. Holloway was with him. Kimbra, who'd driven Jeff's friends to the hospital, sat next to Lacey and DJ stood staring out the lone window that overlooked the hospital parking lot.

Josh was back at the House, waiting for word and consoling the boys from Jeff's room. Katie shook her head to clear it of the angry words she and Josh were having when the news about Jeff had come. They'd parted in mid-argument. Katie realized that they'd solved nothing, but right now, all she wanted to think about was Jeff and comforting her friends.

"How long before they tell us something?" Lacey asked. Her voice sounded tight and scared. "It's been over two hours since the ambulance brought him in."

"I don't know," Kimbra said. "We have to be patient."

"I don't do 'patient' well."

Kimbra patted Lacey's hand. "I'm anxious about him too." She stood. "I'll run down to ER and see if Richard knows anything. You all wait here."

Kimbra left and Lacey made a beeline for DJ. "How could you have let something like this happen? You knew Jeff has hemophilia. You knew how risky it is for him to have a bleeding episode."

DJ looked startled by Lacey's vehemence.

Chelsea came quickly to his aid. "Don't blame DJ. I'm sure it wasn't his fault."

"How do you know? He's responsible for the horses. He should have been watching more carefully."

Katie slipped into the foray, putting herself between Lacey and DJ. "Yelling at each other won't help," she said.

DJ glared at Lacey over Katie's shoulder. "It wasn't anybody's fault. I was washing down one of the horses and Jeff came by to talk. I think a horsefly bit the animal just as Jeff was walking around him. The horse kicked and connected with Jeff. It was an accident."

"An accident that could cause him to bleed to death!"

Chelsea gasped. "Lacey, that's not fair. Don't blame DJ."

DJ shoved away from the window and the group. "I don't need you dumping on me about this. I feel rotten about it. Jeff's a friend and there's no way I want anything bad to happen to him." He glared at Chelsea, his eyes troubled, his lips pressed into a line. "And I don't need you defending me. I can take care of myself."

The three girls watched him stalk out of the waiting room.

"I'm sure he didn't mean to snap at you," Katie told Chelsea hastily, seeing the pained expression on her face. "He was just reacting." She turned to Lacey, adding, "Just like you were reacting. Honestly, Lacey, surely you know DJ's not to blame for Jeff's accident."

Lacey hunkered down and swiped at tears in her eyes. "I'm mad, that's all. I guess I shouldn't have taken it out on DJ. He was handy and he was there when it happened. It shouldn't have even happened." She directed her attention toward Chelsea. "It's just that this is so serious, you know?"

Chelsea said nothing, but Katie could tell she was still smarting from DJ's remark to her. Why had he taken out his frustration on poor Chelsea, Katie wondered. Couldn't he tell how much she cared about him?

Katie and Chelsea walked Lacey back to her chair and they settled on a blue upholstered settee across from the chair. In one corner a TV set was turned to an afternoon soap opera. The volume was low, the actors' voices barely audible. "I don't know much about hemophilia," Katie admitted. "Do you?"

Lacey sniffed and nodded. "I've read up on it. I figured that since Jeff's a part of my life, I should know about his medical problems."

"Tell us about it." Katie was curious, but she also knew it would be a good thing to keep Lacey's mind off time crawling past as they waited for word about Jeff.

"His blood lacks some clotting factor. The factor's found in blood plasma and the sooner he gets this stuff into him, the better the chance of stopping the bleeding and putting off damage."

"What kind of damage?"

"Well, if he bleeds internally, which is what's happening now, the blood makes him swell, and if it doesn't clot, he'll bleed to death."

"But if they give him the clotting factor, won't that stop the bleeding?"

"Yes, but he's still got all this blood from the injury inside him. It has to go somewhere. He got kicked on the thigh. His leg was already horribly swollen by the time the ambulance arrived. I saw it. The medic had to cut away Jeff's jeans because his leg was so swollen."

"I saw them pack his leg in ice," Katie said. "That'll keep the swelling down."

"That helps some, but he's got to get that clotting factor into him in an IV."

"I'm sure they're doing that now down in ER."

"Then once the bleeding's under control, they have to get rid of the clotted blood inside his leg. If they don't dissolve it, it could be life threatening. Sometimes the blood settles into joints and over time can cause arthritis."

Katie saw the complexity of his medical situation and marveled over the way he'd managed to maintain the semblance of a normal life every day. She recalled his thoughtful nature and friendly smile. "I'm sure he'll be all right."

"He'd better be," Lacey said, glaring at the spot by the window where DJ had stood.

It was another fifteen minutes before Kimbra came back into the waiting room. She looked tired, but less worried. "They're getting the bleeding under control," she told the girls. "And they've talked to his hematologist in Miami."

"Thank God," Chelsea said.

"I want to see him," Lacey insisted. "When can I see him?"

"Soon. They're going to send him upstairs and check him into a room."

"For how long?" Lacey looked dismayed.

"The ER doctor said it'll take at least twenty-four hours for the clotting factor to stop the bleeding. After that, if no new bleeding occurs at the site, it may take five days to a week for his leg to return to normal. They'll keep Jeff under observation for at least three or four days and if he looks good, they'll release him. But he'll have to use crutches for maybe another week."

"But he's going to be okay?"

Kimbra put her arm around Lacey's waist. "We'll know better in a couple of days." She looked around. "Where's DJ?"

"He—um—went downstairs. I'm sure he'll be back soon."

"I'm going to call Jenny House and give them an update," Kimbra said. "I know everyone's worried about Jeff. When DJ returns ask him to stay put. I don't want to lose track of any of you."

In another fifteen minutes, DJ returned. Katie spied a Band-Aid taped over a cotton ball in the inner side of his elbow. "What's that for?"

"I donated blood to Jeff's cause," DJ said with a scowl at Lacey. "I figured it was the least I could do."

The three girls traded glances. Katie knew that they couldn't do the same for Jeff because of their medical problems. "It was nice of you," she said.

Chelsea nodded, scared to say anything. Afraid DJ might go off on her again.

Minutes later, Kimbra returned to say that Jeff had just been put in a private room down the hall. The group hurried down the long corridor to gather outside his closed door. "Me first," Lacey announced.

Katie stepped aside with the others, figuring that Lacey did have the most right to visit with him before herself and the others. "Don't start a fight with him," Katie mumbled to Lacey under her breath.

"I won't. But I am nervous. We haven't exactly been on friendly terms lately." Lacey tossed her mane of blond hair and stepped through the door-way.

Jeff lay in a hospital bed, his leg elevated and loosely covered with the bedsheet. His tangle of brown hair spilled across his forehead and seemed a stark contrast to the clean white pillow. An IV pole stood on the far side of the bed and bags of clear liquid hung down. Plastic tubing draped downward and was taped against his forearm. She knew from experience that an IV needle had been threaded into his vein. Lacey calmed the butterflies in her stomach and approached the side of his bed. "Hi."

He turned his head toward her. "Hi yourself."

She noticed that he didn't offer her a smile. "I'll bet your leg hurts."

He said nothing.

"I've been worried about you."

His lips pressed together and his eyes regarded her warily. She allowed her gaze to trace along the IV lines. Jeff followed the path her gaze took. Finally, he said, "Take a good long look, Lacey. Because this is how it is for me. This is how it's always going to be. Except that someday they won't be able to stop the bleeding."

"I know what's happening to you," she said with a defiant lift of her chin. "I understand the facts of your life."

"I'll bet." He balled the bedsheet in his fists. "Now that you've seen me, go away. Go away and leave me alone. You see, I don't want you in my life any more than you want me in yours."

Sixteen

THE TONE OF hostility in Jeff's voice unnerved Lacey. She'd learned long ago that *what* a person said wasn't nearly so meaningful as the *way* it was said. "I never said I wanted you out of my life," she told him.

"Correction—your wording was, 'I want you out of my life, period.'" When she didn't respond, he asked, "Did I misquote you or something? Because if I did, I'll apologize."

Lacey felt her face flush crimson. Of course, he'd quoted her exactly. "All right, I did say it. But I didn't *mean* it."

"Then why did you say it?"

She squirmed, hating to be on the defensive. "I was angry. Haven't you ever said something you didn't mean when you got angry? Or are you perfect?"

"Don't go trying to turn the tables on me, Lacey. Don't try and make me the fall guy in this."

She wanted to give him a tongue-lashing, but seeing him stretched out on the bed, looking helpless, curbed her anger. She sighed. "I didn't come in here to fight with you, Jeff. I don't like fighting with you. I—I've been worried sick about you. I just want you to be all right."

The angry scowl left his face and all at once he looked tired and drained. "And I didn't mean to blast you either. I guess this whole incident caught me off guard. I've been feeling really good this summer. Sometimes I forget about my condition. I try and be so careful . . . and then, out of the blue, I get kicked by a horse. Go figure."

She was relieved that they weren't shouting at each other. "My diabetes catches me off guard sometimes too," she said. "Let me forget one meal and I have an insulin reaction. Then I get reminded all over again that it's a part of me. Remember last spring when you visited me in the hospital?"

"I remember."

"You told me that I had to make peace with my diabetes. That I had to work out some kind of peaceful coexistence or it would destroy me. I've never forgotten what you said. And I am taking care of myself." She reached out and covered his hand resting on the sheet. Touching him felt good and natural and she realized all over again how much he meant to her. Why couldn't she communicate that to him? Why did they always end up fighting? "I'd do anything for you, Jeff. All you have to do is ask."

"I know you're grateful to me because I stuck by you when you were in the hospital. Which is more than any girl has ever done when she sees me like this." He gestured toward the IV line. "I am glad you're here." He glanced toward the closed door. "Did any others come?"

Lacey remembered Katie, Chelsea, and DJ waiting in the hall. Still, she was reluctant to let them in just yet. There was so much more she wanted to say to Jeff. "Yes, they're outside."

"DJ too?"

She nodded.

"I want them to come in. I especially want DJ to know he's not to blame for this."

Lacey felt a twinge of guilt, remembering how she'd blasted DJ in the waiting room. "I'm sure he's figured it out."

"Tell them to come in," Jeff said. She hesitated, and Jeff added, "We'll talk more later. I know things aren't settled between us."

Lacey opened the door, allowing their friends to enter. Once they surmised that Jeff was truly doing well, they joked with him, staying on until a nurse told them visiting hours were over. Kimbra drove everyone back to Jenny House, where they arrived in time for dinner. Lacey ate quickly, put away her tray, and left the cafeteria. She had something to take care of and she didn't want to put it off any longer.

She made her way down to the stables in the darkness. A soft breeze stirred in the pine trees and carried the scent of wild mountain flowers. She félt a deep sense of longing for Jeff and thought of him confined to his hospital bed. She was sorry they'd fought that afternoon. Why couldn't she make him understand what she felt for him? How could she make him see that while she hated his hemophiliac condition, it didn't change the way she felt about him as a person? She disliked *all* sickness; she wasn't discriminating against his. She sighed, tired of wrestling with the problem.

The stables came into sight and she reminded herself of what she'd come to do. As she walked along the front of the stables, curious horses poked their heads over the open half-doors of their stalls and pricked their ears forward. Some snickered and neighed softly, flaring their nostrils to catch her scent. She continued on to the lighted tack room at the end of the barn. At the closed door, she paused and rapped gently.

"Who's there?" DJ asked.

"Lacey Duval." She entered the room and saw DJ sitting on a stool working on a saddle with paste wax and a rag. He looked up, surprise registering on his face. "What are you doing?" she asked.

"Soaping a saddle. It keeps the leather supple." He eyed her cautiously. "Do you need something?"

"You didn't come to dinner tonight."

"I decided to eat here at the stables."

"Are the horses better company than people?"

"Sometimes."

She cleared her throat. "Listen, I came to say I'm sorry for the way I lit into you at the hospital this afternoon. I know it really wasn't your fault that Jeff got kicked. I—um—was mad about the accident and spouted off without thinking." She offered a sly smile. "My friends who know me say this is one tiny weeny flaw of mine—I sometimes speak without thinking. I do a lot of apologizing for it."

DJ listened attentively, then returned to buffing the saddle. "No problem. I didn't take offense."

She had more to say and wondered how best to broach the subject of Chelsea with him. "Are you having a good time this summer?"

"It's okay."

"Just okay?"

"I should be back home helping on the ranch. We'll be driving the cattle down from the upper ranges in another month. It's a big job and Dad needs all the hands he can get."

"We'll all be home again in another month, so you should be able to help." She wandered over to where he worked and fingered bridles hanging on hooks along the wall. "I met Jillian. I liked her."

DJ stopped buffing at the mention of his sister. "When did you meet her?"

"Last November, when she and Katie and Chelsea flew up in your father's private plane. Katie had sent me air fare, and Mr. Holloway and I met their plane when it landed. We stayed at Jenny House together over the holiday."

DJ went back to his work.

"I didn't want to like her, you know. I thought she was an intruder into my friendships with Katie and Chelsea. But no matter how hard I tried to not like her, it didn't work."

"Yeah, everybody liked Jillian."

"I think that's because she liked everybody. She even liked me." DJ gave her a questioning look and she smiled candidly. "I know I can grate on people's nerves sometimes."

"Sometimes," he said.

"Do you know who she liked best of all though?"

"Who?"

"Chelsea." She saw him tense at the mention of the name. "That's why it would probably bother the stew out of her if she knew how *you* were treating Chelsea."

"What do you mean? I treat Chelsea fine."

"You treat her like a criminal."

"Now wait a minute—"

"No. It's about time someone told you how much you're hurting Chelsea by the way you're ignoring her." Lacey hadn't raised her voice. She kept it steady and matter-of-fact. "You leave the room every time she comes in. You don't speak to her unless she speaks first. You're downright rude. Why do you suppose you act that way toward her?"

"I treat her the way I do everybody else."

"No, you don't. Do you want to know what I think?"

He was beginning to look angry. "Not particularly."

She ignored his answer. "I think you're mad at her because she lived and your sister died."

"I know it wasn't her fault she got transplanted and Jillian didn't. I don't blame Chelsea."

"Maybe you know it up here." She tapped her finger against his temple. "But you don't believe it right here." She placed her hand on his shirtfront, against his heart. "Don't feel bad; I've read that it's a common problem among survivors."

"Survivors?"

"Yeah . . . the people left behind when a person they love dies. Anyway, you've been less than nice to Chelsea, and it's hurting her feelings. And I'm mentioning it to you so that you can make it up to her."

He stood and heaved the saddle onto the floor. "For starters, I don't know how to make something up to Chelsea when I don't know what I'm doing wrong. And besides that, I've got plenty to do to keep me busy here at the stables. I don't have time to hang around up at Jenny House making friends with the visitors."

"Chelsea isn't just a visitor," Lacey corrected. "She was Jillian's best friend. And she deserves better treatment from you." She watched his jaw clench, but he didn't lash out at her. "So, anyway, that's what I came down here to say. I mean, after I told you I was sorry about blaming you for Jeff's accident." Still, DJ said nothing. "Guess I'll be going now." Lacey walked to the doorway, where she paused. "Will you think about what I said?"

"I'll think about it."

"Believe me, DJ, your being nice to Chelsea is what Jillian would have wanted." Lacey stepped outside, released her bottled-up tension in one long breath, then started up the trail leading to the House. She felt pleased. Satisfied that she'd spoken her mind without getting angry or overly sarcastic. *Good job,* she told herself as she walked along. Now if only she could deal with Jeff in the same dispassionate manner. But dealing with Jeff was never easy for her. The problem there was that she was in love with Jeff. And it was hard for her to remain neutral when her heart was at stake.

I'll find a way, she thought. *I will!*

Seventeen

"I THINK WE should throw a party for him," Chelsea said. She and her friends were sitting at the breakfast table debating the best way to welcome Jeff home from his week-long stay at the hospital. "I remember how special I felt when you gave me that surprise birthday party last summer."

"I don't know," Lacey said. "Last night when I visited Jeff, he told me all he wanted to do was come back and get to work without any fanfare. Besides, he's on crutches and a party might be awkward. I mean, what can he do except sit around watching everybody else have fun?"

"So what?" Katie piped in. "Since when did you ever do exactly what someone asked?"

"I'm turning over a new leaf," Lacey protested. "Especially with Jeff."

Chelsea traded glances with Katie. "The kids in his room want to throw a party too," Chelsea said. "They've talked to me about it and I don't think we should disappoint them. They like Jeff a lot and they've missed him."

"Kimbra says she'll special-order a cake. Come on. It'll be fun." Katie fidgeted in her chair. Warm August sunlight flooded through the windows, turning the paper tablecloth a brilliant, sun-washed shade of white.

"He may not like it," Lacey warned.

"He'll love it," Katie said, snatching up her tray. "We'll plan more later. Right now, I have to take a group down to the pool for swimming."

From the corner of her eye, Chelsea saw Josh heading toward their table and wondered if Katie's sudden departure was due entirely to group swimming. It was obvious to her that something was wrong between the two of them. Katie was purposefully avoiding Josh.

Lost in her own thoughts, Lacey hadn't noticed anything. "If Jeff bites my head off, I'm telling him this wasn't my idea," she grumbled.

"And if he loves it, you can take full credit," Chelsea said. "Which you probably will anyway." She observed Josh attempt to stop Katie's retreat from the cafeteria and saw her friend brush him off. The wounded expression on his face tugged at Chelsea's heartstrings. "Let's talk about this later," she said, standing and picking up her tray.

"Why is everyone running off?"

"Places to go. People to see," Chelsea said with a big smile.

"Thanks a bunch. Leave me alone to organize all the details." Lacey hunched down in her chair and Chelsea hurried toward Josh.

"Wait up," she called. "Where're you headed?"

"No place, it seems." He was still looking at the doorway through which Katie had fled.

"Want to take a walk with me?"

"I won't be much company."

"Oh, come on. I need my exercise."

They went outside into the escalating summer heat. The leaves lay limp and listless on the trees and the air felt hot and heavy on Chelsea's skin. She chose a hiking trail, wandering down the path slowly with a reluctant Josh. Sounds of laughter coming from the pool shattered the green stillness of the woods. They walked in silence, with Chelsea taking covert sidelong glances at Josh's troubled face until she finally worked up the courage to ask, "Want to talk about it?"

"About what?"

"You and Katie. I know something's wrong between you two." He said nothing. She persisted. "I know her better than anybody, Josh. I lived with her while waiting for my transplant, remember? I can read her like a book and I know when something's bothering her. And I know when something's bothering you too."

His shoulders slumped and he stopped walking. "I'm losing her."

"How do you mean?"

He told her briefly about their ongoing discussion of Katie's going away to college. And of how much he wanted her to stay in Michigan and be with him.

"We all know about the scholarship offer," Chelsea said. "What I don't understand is why you think she'll forget you and all that you've meant to each other simply because she takes it."

"Come on. Katie's a real babe. She'll get out there and forget all about me."

"How do you figure that?"

He took his time answering. "Do you know about Garrison?"

"A little."

"She was interested in him. Really interested. I got jealous and made her stay away from him, but I know she'd have dated him if I hadn't acted like a pit bull."

Chelsea smiled at his description of himself. "Katie's pretty headstrong. If Garrison really meant that much to her, she'd have dated him."

"Did you know he came up here a few weeks ago and saw her?"

Chelsea hadn't known because Katie hadn't told her. It bothered her, but she didn't want to let on to Josh. "So what? She didn't run off with him, did she?"

Her reasoning didn't appear to comfort him. He tossed back his head and stared up at patches of blue sky through the tree branches. "All we do anymore is fight, Chelsea. I want things to be like they used to be. Like when she was in the hospital and training for the Transplant Olympic Games. Things were good then. She loved me then."

The soft wistful longing in his voice almost brought tears to Chelsea's eyes. "She still loves you. She just wants to *live* a little. Go after her dreams."

"And I'm standing in her way. Is that it? I have dreams too, you know. And they all center around Katie."

Chelsea felt a twinge of envy. Why couldn't a boy feel that way toward her? "Maybe that's the problem," Chelsea offered, focusing again on Josh. "Maybe it would be better if you had other plans and dreams too. I don't think anybody likes to feel that she's somebody else's purpose for living. It can make a person feel hemmed in. You know?"

"But I don't know what else to want, except Katie."

"You ran track too, didn't you?"

"Sure, but I was never a star. I don't have the talent she has."

"You're going to college though, aren't you?"

"I'll have to work and I'll be living with Gramps, but yes, I'm going. I won't be able to take a full course load either. And I have no idea what I'll major in."

"All Katie wants to do is *run*, Josh. In four years, it'll be over for her. Then she can be with you."

"But what if something happens to her? What if her transplant rejects—?" He stopped, mid-sentence, realizing who he was talking to.

"It's all right," Chelsea said. "Katie and I live with that possibility every day. We know that anything over five years is a bonus for us."

"And she's already had her heart for two years." Josh sounded impassioned. "Four years away at college will be four years less I have to spend with her. She's already living on borrowed time."

"Who isn't?" Chelsea said quietly. "Did your brother expect to die so soon? Or Amanda and Jillian?"

He shook his head sadly. Chelsea took a deep breath and continued. "Katie and I both know the odds we face. If we lived every day in fear of the odds, we'd never accomplish anything. I know what it is to live scared, Josh. It's not much fun. I'm trying hard to be more daring, more adventurous It's an everyday struggle, but it's worth it to me."

"It's hard to let her go." His voice was a fervent whisper.

She tipped her head thoughtfully. "I spent many years too sick to do anything—not even leave my bedroom. I read a lot. Books, and the places they took me, became my only escape."

"Until you discovered Virtual Reality."

She smiled. "Katie introduced me. But, even now, books are some of my best friends. And I read something once that's always stuck with me. It was a proverb or something. It said, 'If you love something, let it go. If it loves you, it'll come back.' What do you think of that saying?"

He studied her for a long time before speaking. "I think the writer of that proverb never loved Katie O'Roark. And never lost the people in his life that he loved. I think that the writer hasn't a clue about how lonely a person feels when the people he loves disappear from his life one by one."

"In my honest opinion, Josh, Katie cares enough about you that you can make her reject the track scholarship."

"Do you really think so?"

Chelsea nodded, though she felt disappointed by the eagerness she heard in his voice. "What you have to decide," she added, "is what's more important to you—your happiness or Katie's."

"I can make Katie happy," Josh insisted. "And once she starts running track for Michigan, she'll forget all about moving off to Arizona. That's what I want her to understand. She has the same opportunities by staying at home that she does by moving away. And you've just helped me see it more clearly." He grinned, and for the first time that morning, he looked relieved. "Thanks, Chelsea. I'm glad we talked."

"Yes, but—"

"Look, I want to get back to the House. Mind if I jog on ahead?"

"No problem," she said. He waved and started up the trail. She felt confused and apprehensive. She'd hoped to help Katie's situation with college and track, and now it seemed that she might have hurt her. The air felt as if it was closing in on her. She took a long shuddering breath. "Oh, Katie," she whispered. "What have I done?"

Eighteen

LACEY DECIDED THAT Jeff's surprise party should be a hayride in the moonlight for all the kids and staff of Jenny House.

"A hayride?" Dullas squawked when she heard the plan that night in their room. She wrinkled her nose. "What a dumb idea."

"Excuse me," Lacey said, eyeing her narrowly. "Since when is any idea of mine dumb? This way Jeff can ride to a place where we'll set up a bonfire, roast hot dogs and marshmallows, and have cake. I only have another couple of weeks to soften him up before we all have to head home. I'm convinced that a nice leisurely ride in the moonlight will give him lots of time to snuggle with me. You're just lucky I'm allowing everybody else to share in the experience."

Dullas bit into an apple, then chucked it into the

wastebasket. "Okay, so it's not such a dumb idea. But what are the rest of us going to do? I mean, some of us don't have boyfriends to snuggle with."

Latika giggled. "Who'd snuggle with you, Dullas? It'd be like curling up with a cactus."

Dullas leaped across the room and balled her fist in Latika's face. "Watch your mouth, creep. I should pound you into the floor."

Latika cowered and Lacey wedged herself between them. It had been so long since Dullas had blown up, she'd forgotten how threatening the girl could be. "Give it a rest."

"You're always taking her side," Dullas shouted. "Why do you like her and not me?"

The girl's tirade caught Lacey totally by surprise. "Calm down. I like you both."

"No, you don't. You hate me and always have. I hate everybody here and I wish I'd never come."

"Two more weeks and you'll get your wish," Lacey said sharply. "Summer at Jenny House will be over."

"Good!" Dullas shoved Latika hard and ran out of the room.

Lacey knelt beside Latika, who'd begun to cry. "I hate her. She's so mean."

"You're not hurt, are you?"

Latika shook her head. Lacey comforted her, all the while wondering what could have possibly set off Dullas. She told herself she shouldn't let it drop, but soon she became so engrossed with the details of the hayride that she didn't think of the incident again until she crawled into bed and saw both girls asleep on the other side of the room. *In the morning*, she told herself sleepily. *I'll talk to her in the morning*.

But the next morning Dullas was gone when Lacey woke up, and right after breakfast Mr. Holloway brought Jeff back from the hospital. The kids from his room almost knocked him off his crutches crowding around him. Lacey stood in the background, savoring the pleasure of his presence. How good he looked! How good to have him well again.

That night, three flatbed trucks loaded with straw pulled up to the front deck. Long hand-painted banners stretched across the sides and read, WELCOME BACK, JEFF! and LET'S PARTY! Balloons were tied in clusters and secured to posts on the trucks. Music played from a tape deck fastened to the top of the lead truck. "Whose idea was this?" Jeff asked, looking flustered.

"It depends on how much you like it," Katie said.

A slow grin spread over his face. "It's all right. It's good to know I was missed."

Lacey stepped forward and waved her hand. "My idea. Any excuse for a party, you know. Glad you like it."

Chelsea and Katie rolled their eyes at one another.

Soon, the groups had divided up and kids and counselors piled into the dry, scratchy straw. The moon had cooperated by rising full and round, and now it glowed in the night sky like a shimmering disk. The trucks drove slowly, taking plenty of time to reach the field where the bonfire was waiting to be lit. Lacey curled up next to Jeff and slid her hand into his. "I'm glad you're here," she said.

Their truck carried kids who horsed around by

stuffing straw down each other's backs and then hopped up and down to dislodge it. No one was paying Jeff and Lacey much mind. "I've hated being in the hospital ever since I was a little kid," he told her. "I wish I never had to go again."

"Well, you know how much fun I had in the hospital," Lacey said drolly.

Jeff gazed up at the moon. "Hard to believe the summer's almost over."

"Are you staying in the same apartment in Miami as last year?" She remembered the wild colors and the way he'd asked her help him redecorate. She now regretted refusing and wanted a second chance.

"I'm not sure."

"Why not?"

"I may not return to Miami at all."

Her heart lurched. "But you're not finished with college yet."

"I'm going home from here—back to Colorado. I need to talk to my folks. Sending me to the University of Miami is expensive. I've been thinking that maybe I should look for a college closer to home."

"But I'd hate that!"

"You'd hate it. Why? You never showed any interest in me while I was living in Miami."

She lost her temper. "Why do I have to keep apologizing for the way I treated you last September? Hasn't this summer proven that I like you, Jeff?"

"Maybe you were bored." He gestured toward the others. "Not too many guys for you to toy with this summer like last year."

She flushed, knowing that was a reason she'd once

given for pairing off with him the sun
"Are you going to throw up every nasty
I've ever said for the rest of my life? I t____ ____, ___
sorry. I talk without thinking."

"And so how do I know what you're saying now is really the truth? How can I trust you, Lacey?"

"I didn't walk out on you when you were in the hospital, did I?" she fired back. "How long are you going to question me about my feelings? How many times do I have to say it? Stop punishing me, Jeff. I know what I want."

He caught the back of her neck and pulled her face within inches of his own. "I know what I want too, Lacey. I know what I've wanted since the first time I laid eyes on you." His voice was low, almost fierce.

She felt her insides turn to jelly. "What? What do you want?"

He gritted his teeth. "I want you, girl. Heaven help me." With that he kissed her soundly, until her mouth fairly sizzled and the old familiar fireworks exploded inside her like a holiday celebration.

"Hey, look!" someone shouted. "Jeff's kissing Lacey!"

"Ow—cooties!" a boy bellowed.

The rest of the kids erupted into catcalls and loud smacking noises.

Lacey didn't care. She threw her arms around Jeff's neck and returned his kiss with all her heart.

Chelsea watched Jeff and Lacey roasting marshmallows over the giant bonfire. Their arms were linked around one another's waists and their faces looked adiant. Obviously, they'd settled their differences and were once more together. *Together*. She sighed. Would there ever be someone special for *her* that way?

"You want a marshmallow?"

DJ's question interrupted her fantasy. She glanced about, to make sure he wasn't addressing someone else.

"I'm asking you, Chelsea," he said quietly.

The way he drawled over the syllables of her name made her knees go weak. "I'm not so crazy about marshmallows," she said, then felt stupid for saying such a dumb thing. What did it matter? "Do you want something?" she asked when she sensed that he seemed hesitant to walk off and leave her.

"Yeah. I want to say I'm sorry if I've hurt your feelings."

"Why do you think you've hurt my feelings?"

"Something someone said to me. Plus I've been doing a lot of thinking. I know I've not been nice to you."

Instantly, she wondered who'd been talking about her to him. She didn't ask, but instead, screwed up her courage and said what was truly on her mind. "I know you resent me for living when Jillian didn't. I can't change that part."

He nodded slowly. "I've tried not to, but you're right. I have been mad at you. I know it's not fair, but it's the way I've been feeling."

His confession wounded her—even though she'd known it was the truth. "So . . . how do I make it up to you?"

They were standing under a tree. He reached up and tugged off a leaf and began to twirl it in his fingers. "Jillian wanted us to be steadies. She worked hard at setting us up."

Chelsea laughed nervously. *So he'd known!* "Silly idea, huh? I tried to tell her it would never work, but she wouldn't listen. Besides, there's always Shelby."

"I told you before, Shelby and I are quits. I didn't like the way she carried on about me not taking her to some Christmas parties. My sister was dying! What did she think I was going to do—fly back home for some stupid party and leave my family?"

Chelsea remembered when he'd visited her in the hospital and brought her Jillian's expensive Monopoly set for a gift. "Jillian left me a videotape to watch after she died," she told DJ. "In it, she said you'd take her loss real hard. She had some idea that I might be able to take care of you." Chelsea dropped her gaze to the ground. "You don't need taking care of—especially by me."

"My sister had a yen for life to turn out happily ever after. She had to work at it sometimes, but she got her way a lot."

"But she didn't get her way with the transplant," Chelsea said, looking him in the eye. "And not with you and me."

"It's nothing personal." He dropped the leaf. She watched it flutter to the hard ground. "You're a good-looking girl, Chelsea. And you're smart and sensitive. It shows all over you. But there's just too much in the way between us. Too much I still have to work out on my own."

She smiled to herself. He had a kind way of dashing a girl's hopes. Maybe it was his southern breeding. Seeing him in the moonlight, watching moonbeams reflect off his blond hair, made her want to kiss him. But not a kiss of passion. More a kiss of goodbye. He was the first boy she'd ever had a crush on. The first boy she'd ever dreamed about and longed for. Because of her lifelong illness, she'd not lived a normal life and she supposed she was light-years behind other girls her age. Her new heart offered her a new life. It was time to say goodbye to her old one once and for all. "I hope you find what you're looking for, DJ," she said.

"You too," he answered.

"I will. Because now I have the time to look."

Their gazes locked, and briefly, time seemed to stand still.

"Chelsea!" Lacey's voice shattered the mood.

Chelsea turned to see Lacey coming toward her. "What is it?"

Lacey's gaze darted between Chelsea and DJ. "Sorry if I'm interrupting anything, but have you seen Dullas? We can't find her anywhere."

Nineteen

"No, I haven't seen Dullas," Chelsea told Lacey. "But then, I haven't been looking for her either."

"Did she even come on the hayride?" DJ asked.

"One of the counselors wanted to know the same thing," Lacey said. "I told her that I thought everybody came, but she reminded me that some staff stayed behind to hold the fort until we got back."

Chelsea offered her opinion. "So maybe Dullas decided to stay behind too. You know how sulky she's been these past couple of days."

"She *has* gotten testy lately," Lacey conceded. "I've been meaning to talk to her about it."

"I don't think I'd worry too much about her," DJ said. "Not coming tonight is her loss."

Still, Lacey wasn't cheered. Jeff came up and took her hand. "None of the guys from my room have seen her. Don't let it get you down. Come on back to the bonfire with me. We'll have some cake."

"I could go for some cake," DJ said.

The four of them walked toward the bonfire, which still smoldered. Several of the staff were busily cutting a sheet cake and passing it out to an eager line of kids. "Any luck?" one of them asked.

"I'm guessing she decided not to come," Lacey said.

"It really wasn't an option for the kids," Janie, one of the nurses, said. "Kimbra stayed behind tonight. When we get back, I'll ask her to have a heart-to-heart talk with Dullas. She should know by now that she can't go off doing her own thing whenever she feels like it."

"Soon we'll all be doing our own things again," Chelsea said. "Isn't that so, Katie?"

Katie looked up, startled. She'd been so deep in thought that she'd barely heard the discussion. "What? Oh, sure. I guess so." She took her paper plate and piece of cake away from the crowd gathered around the glowing fire. She crawled up onto the back of one of the trucks, parked in the open field, and settled into the straw. Overhead the moon glimmered down, but its light made her feel lonely and isolated.

Minutes later, Josh found her. "Can I join you?"

She dreaded another confrontation, but this time she was prepared. She'd made up her mind to take the scholarship. The day before, she'd called and told her parents what she wanted to do. They'd put forth their familiar arguments, but she'd countered every one, and in the end, they'd agreed. She'd dropped a letter in the mail that afternoon telling the Arizona coach of her decision. Now she had to tell Josh. She steeled herself for what was going to be the hardest thing she'd ever done.

"Sure, join me." She patted the straw and he climbed up beside her.

"Nice night."

"Every night in these mountains is nice."

His long legs dangled over the side of the truck while she sat cross-legged. He turned his face toward her. "You know we have to talk, Katie." She nodded. "Things between us have been coming to a head all summer."

"But it's still been a great summer."

"It has. Are you still mad because I invited myself to Jenny House? I've worked hard, you know."

"I know—and no, I'm not mad."

"But you said you wanted time to think, and I know I crowded you even though I tried hard not to."

She took a deep breath, felt the palms of her hands turn clammy with apprehension. "I have had time to think."

"Me too."

She regarded him warily. "What have you thought about? New arguments to get me to stay in Ann Arbor?"

"Mostly." He rotated his shoulders, as if shedding great tension. "But that's not what I'm going to say right now."

"What do you mean?"

"I'm not going to try and persuade you to stay. I've decided that you should take the scholarship offer and go."

"Did I hear you correctly? You want me to go?"

"Don't look so shocked," Josh said, lifting her chin. "I don't like it, Katie, but I know it's something that you have to do. I'm through trying to force you to give it up. It's not right."

"Why did you change your mind?"

"A lot of little things—like the time you asked me about Aaron's dreams. But it was Jeff's bleeding episode that brought things into focus for me. Nobody knows how much time they have. And there's no way a person can plan for the unexpected. So it makes sense to plan for the things you really want. And if they happen"—he shrugged—"they happen. All your life, you planned to run and win. Your transplant was a real setback, but you never gave up. It wouldn't be fair of me to make you give up now after you've overcome so many other obstacles to get what you want."

"Josh . . . I—I don't know what to say."

"Say you'll write me. And that you won't forget me."

"Never!" She threw her arms around his neck.

He hugged her so tightly, it took her breath away. "One more thing." He pulled back. "And this is the hardest thing of all for me to say."

Her heart hammered as she watched emotion cross his face in the moonlight, but she let him take his time. So far, he'd offered her more than she'd imagined possible and she was grateful.

"I think," he began quietly, "it would be best," he pulled a piece of straw from her hair, "if we date other people next year."

She almost slid off the truck. "But why? I don't want to date anybody else."

"You will, Katie." He caught her gaze. "It's all right. You should date other guys."

"Why are you doing this, Josh? *What* are you doing?"

"I'm letting you go," he said with a sad smile.

"Feels more like you're trying to get rid of me."

He shook his head. "Girls are such a mystery—one I'll never figure out. Listen, you know how I feel about you. Time and distance isn't going to change that for me. But you're the one who needs to know what *you* want. And *who* you want."

She swallowed against a lump that had formed in her throat. "Does this mean you're taking back your marriage proposal?"

"Let's just say I'm putting it in storage for a while."

Automatically, her hand went to her neck and her fingers closed around the heart-shaped pendant. "Do you want this back?"

"Of course not. But when you get out to Arizona, take it off and put it away. Have a good time. And run like the wind."

A tear slid down her cheek. She had prepared herself for arguing and fighting. She'd equipped herself for dealing with his anger and frustration. What she hadn't prepared for was this kindness, this gentle giving and self-sacrifice. "I love you, Josh."

His arms went around her again and he held her

against his body. "I love you, Katie. Ever since that first time I saw you in ICU, hooked up to all those machines, when you turned your head, opened your eyes, and stared straight into mine. I started loving you then. And I've never stopped."

Shakily, she pulled away and wiped the back of her hand across her eyes. "You made everything possible for me. Thank you. For Aaron's heart. For tonight. I *will* come home to you, Josh. I promise."

He smoothed his fingertips over her cheek. "We'll see." He jumped down off the truck. "Let's go roast a marshmallow. Have some fun."

He lifted her down and held her again. Then, hand in hand, they headed toward the bonfire and sounds of laughter. They hadn't gone far when Katie looked eastward and noticed a red glow in the sky. She stopped and pointed. "Josh, what's that?"

He squinted. "Don't know."

"It's near Jenny House."

"Yeah . . . Come on." He tugged her hand and together they jogged toward the group. They found Janie eating cake with several of the kids. Josh pointed out the strange red hue on the horizon. "What do you think it is?"

Janie stood. Her hand went to her throat. "It looks like a fire," she whispered. "Oh no! Jenny House is on fire!"

Twenty

∽

T HE NEXT FEW hours passed like a nightmare for Katie. There was a quick smothering of the bonfire and frightened kids piling onto the trucks for the dash back to Jenny House. The distant sound of the mournful wail of fire trucks, making their way up the secluded road toward the fire, pierced the night.

"This can't be happening," Chelsea cried as the flatbed truck bounced along. "Tell me it's a bad dream."

Lacey held on to Jeff and Josh hugged Katie. The trucks were going faster than on the leisurely ride to the open field, but to Katie still they seemed to be crawling. At last, the vehicles pulled into the parking lot, a safe distance from the flames, and parked. Katie saw fire trucks with their red lights glaring and hoses sending out arcs of water onto the flaming roof of the building. She watched fire spread onto the wide wooden deck and flames shoot from an upper-story window.

The staff consoled and comforted the frightened kids while firemen yelled, wood crackled, and water hitting flames hissed. "The trees!" yelled one fire-fighter. "Douse them good."

Sprays of water soaked nearby trees while men chopped down the ones nearest the blaze in order to keep it from spreading to the woods. The flames danced bright and angry in the night sky and soot settled everywhere.

Horrified, Katie watched Jenny House burn, tears streaming down her cheeks. "How could this have happened?"

Josh grimly shook his head. "It was a new build-ing. This shouldn't be happening."

"Was there anyone inside?" Katie overheard a fire-man ask. He'd come over to their truck and was talk-ing to one of the staff.

New fears shot through Katie. Where was Kimbra? And Mr. Holloway? And what about Dullas? Had *she* stayed back at the house? If so, where was she now?

"There were a few of the staff in the building when we left for our hayride," the staffer, Janie, told the firefighter. "I don't see them— Wait! There's our di-rector."

Janie pointed, and Katie saw Mr. Holloway coming toward them from the woods. He had Kimbra and Dullas with him. Katie felt her knees go weak with relief.

"Is everyone okay?" Richard Holloway asked.

Janie assured him that all were accounted for.

"We need to get the kids to town," he said.

The fireman radioed for help and soon police sirens could be heard coming up the side of the mountain.

The next hours passed in a blur, but eventually, everyone got into town and settled into the largest hotel. Local businesses, the Red Cross, and churches rallied to help the kids with sleepwear, toothbrushes, and phone calls home. Counselors were assigned rooms, and Katie and her friends found themselves aiding, consoling, and tucking in the residents of Jenny House for the night. Once most were settled and asleep, Mr. Holloway called an emergency staff and personnel meeting in one of the hotel's conference rooms.

"It's a disaster," he told his weary workers. "I understand the fire's out, but we won't be able to evaluate how much damage was suffered until daylight. The important thing is that all the children are safe. Thanks to all of you for your herculean efforts tonight."

Jeff sat next to Lacey, Josh beside Katie. Chelsea clutched the arms of her chair and DJ leaned against the back wall. Soot smudged Kimbra's face.

Someone asked, "Do we know what caused the fire?"

"Not yet. The fire marshal will be able to survey the situation better tomorrow. Needless to say, this is going to end our summer camp prematurely."

Katie felt Josh squeeze her hand.

Mr. Holloway continued, his voice grim and exhausted. "A temporary hospital is being set up in another conference room for those on medications. Hometown doctors are being called to get doses. How many of you need medicine?"

Katie, Chelsea, and Lacey raised their hands. The full horror of the situation struck Katie. She and Chelsea needed their antirejection drugs and Lacey needed insulin.

"Write down what you need," Mr. Holloway said, "and I'll be sure you get it immediately." He raked his fingers through his disheveled blond hair. "I think we all should get some sleep for now. Tomorrow's going to be a long day. We'll be making arrangements to send kids home. If you need anything —and I mean *anything*—here's the phone number of my room. Call, no matter what the time."

He gave the number, a few more instructions, and the meeting broke up. Josh, Jeff, and DJ headed straight upstairs to their rooms and their responsibilities with the younger boys. Katie and her friends headed to the hospital-conference room, where a doctor and two nurses were setting up a table to dispense medicine. Katie and Chelsea took their pills and Lacey drew up her bedtime insulin dose. She asked, "What if we were in a plane crash out in the wilderness or something? Even if we survived the crash, we'd die because we wouldn't have our medications. I *hate* being dependent on medical science."

"Don't rebel now," Katie told her. "We need your help."

They walked out to the lobby, where police and a few reporters interviewing Mr. Holloway were gathered. Katie thought about the nice clean bed upstairs and longed to close her eyes. She heard Lacey say, "Well, Chelsea, it seems your premonition was correct."

"What premonition?"

"You remember—the one you had that day we went up to visit the memorial together."

It came back to Chelsea in a flash. She recalled the chill that had come over her, the dark sense of foreboding she'd felt. "I—I didn't see this kind of disaster."

"You know, you've always had a sixth sense. You said you thought something bad was going to happen, and it did."

"I wonder what started the fire," Katie said. "Josh reminded me that the building was practically new. You'd think it would be pretty much fireproof."

"Yes, I wonder *what*." Lacey crossed her arms and anger clouded her face. "Or who."

For a moment, no one spoke as the implications of Lacey's comment sank in. Chelsea was the first to break the ominous quiet. "That's a pretty rude accusation, Lacey."

"Well, why not?" Lacey whipped around to face her two friends in the corner of the lobby. "Dullas probably has the know-how. Her father's an arsonist, for heaven's sake."

"My father's a sportswriter," Katie said. "And I couldn't write a column if my life depended on it."

"You know her best, Lacey," Chelsea said. "You should know if she's capable of such a thing."

"I know she's unpredictable and barely civilized.

She's been mean and nasty all week to everyone, and I know she wasn't with us on the hayride."

Katie felt troubled. "Gee, I don't know . . ."

"Well, I know one way to find out." Lacey marched over to the elevator and punched the button.

Katie and Chelsea rushed to her side. "What are you going to do?" Katie wanted to know.

"I'm going upstairs and find Dullas and ask her."

Chelsea started, "Lacey, I don't think you should."

"Why not? I want to know the truth. She's in room 908. I saw it on Mr. Holloway's assignment sheet." The elevator opened and Lacey punched the ninth-floor button. She was breathing heavily and the sound filled the small compartment.

At the door of room 908, Katie grabbed Lacey's elbow. "Wait a minute. Before you go barging in there, think what you're doing. For weeks, you've been Dullas's biggest advocate. You're the one who went to bat for her with Mr. Holloway. How can you accuse her of such a thing as burning down Jenny House?"

Lacey jutted her chin stubbornly. "Maybe that's the reason—I fought for her harder than anyone and I want to know it was worth the effort."

"You can't go upsetting the other girls in the room," Chelsea said when Lacey reached for the doorknob.

"I'll bring her out into the hall," Lacey said, entering the room.

Chelsea chewed her lip nervously and stared hard at Katie. "What if Dullas confesses?"

"Then we'll have to tell Mr. Holloway."

Minutes later, Lacey emerged with a sleepy-eyed Dullas in tow. The younger girl rubbed her eyes at the glare of the hall lights. "What's wrong?"

"That's what we want to know," Lacey said. "Where were you tonight?"

Dullas looked startled, confused. The nightgown she wore was much too big, making her resemble a dwarf. Her bald head looked pale and vulnerable without its customary baseball hat. "What do you mean, where was I? I've been asleep in bed."

"Not now," Lacey said. "Earlier. While we were all on the hayride."

"Aw, let me go back to bed, Lacey. Can't we talk tomorrow?"

Lacey took a firm hold of Dullas's shoulders. "We want to talk now and we want to know why you didn't come on the hayride tonight."

" 'Cause I didn't feel like it." Dullas pushed Lacey's hands off her shoulders. " 'Cause I had something else to do."

"Like what? Start a fire?"

Dullas's mouth dropped open and she glanced from face to face. "You think *I* started the fire?"

"That's what we want to know," Lacey demanded.

"You lousy creeps!" Dullas backed away. "You're serious, aren't you?"

"Look, Dullas, don't be mad—" Chelsea held out her hand with her plea.

"Well, I ain't saying nothing to you! You're creeps and freaks! I hate all of you!"

Katie grew alarmed as Dullas's voice rose. She sure

didn't want to wake up everybody on the floor. "We can talk about this tomorrow—"

"Drop dead!" Dullas spat. "I never want to see any of you again!" She spun and ran back inside the room.

"That didn't go too well," Chelsea said.

"It could be a smoke screen," Lacey declared.

Just then, the elevator slid open and Kimbra stepped into the hall. She looked worn out, but she brightened when she saw the three girls. "Good, you haven't gone to bed yet."

"We were on our way," Katie told her, hoping they didn't look overly guilt-stricken.

"With all the goings-on tonight, I haven't had a chance to tell you something."

"Tell us what?" Lacey asked.

"I've decided to take Dullas home with me. You know, be her foster parent. I know it's a big step, but she was excited once we discussed it. Are you glad?"

Twenty-one

❦

"YOU'RE TAKING DULLAS to live with you?" Katie asked, dumbfounded.

"Why not? The kid needs a break. I talked to my husband, explained about Dullas, and he said it was fine with him." She smiled. "He's a good man and he'll be a good dad to Dullas. Tonight, I told her what we wanted to do. I asked her not to go on the hayride so we could talk—you know, see if she even wanted to move in with us. It took some persuading that I really wanted her, but she does want to come home with me. You know how she tries to act so tough, but she was pleased. I could tell."

"So she was with you when the fire broke out?" Katie didn't cast glances toward Lacey or Chelsea. She didn't want to offer a hint of suspicion to Kimbra about what they'd done.

"We were sitting in the lobby when the smoke alarms went off. Richard came running out of his office and cleared us out. The lobby was filling with smoke as we were running out the door." Kimbra's eyes grew wide as she described the scene. "I shudder to think what could have happened if everyone hadn't been on that hayride. It was a brilliant idea, Lacey. Probably saved many from injury."

"We were lucky," Lacey mumbled.

"I'd say." Kimbra smiled. "I know you all must be exhausted. I sure am. Go on to bed now. We're going to have a mountain of work tomorrow and tonight's half gone."

When she had left, Katie turned and glared straight at Lacey. "What now, Lacey? How are you going to make this up to Dullas?"

Lacey frowned, her pretty face a dark mask. "I'm not sure yet, but I'll think of something."

"You'd better. I'd say we owe Dullas a big-time apology. And I mean *big time*."

The next few days were frenetic as arrangements were made to get kids home. News came that the fire had started in an elevator shaft because of faulty wiring. The sprinkler system had gone off and saved many of the rooms on the upper floors from the fire; therefore most of the kids' belongings were spared, although soaked and soggy. The smell of smoke clung to clothing, and Katie and her friends spent afternoons at the laundrette washing, drying, and folding clothes for the younger ones.

Dullas steered clear of them and Katie and her friends let her be. But late one night, after the few remaining kids were put to bed, Katie said to Lacey, "Josh and I are heading back to Ann Arbor day after tomorrow."

"Jeff and I are leaving for Miami then too. He'll drive me home, then catch a plane for Colorado, but he says he'll be back in September."

"Chelsea's plane leaves in two days," Katie added.

"So what's your point?"

"My point is that we still haven't made up to Dullas."

Lacey nodded. "I know. I've been thinking about it a lot."

"And?"

"And I think I've finally come up with a plan."

Lacey begged Kimbra to take them back to Jenny House for one final look. She drove them, along with Dullas, who didn't seem happy wedged between Lacey and Katie in the backseat. Once at the House, they stared in dismay at the blackened deck, shattered windows, and charred walls. The massive stone fireplace was black with soot. "I can't believe it," Chelsea said, tears filling her eyes.

Katie felt sick to her stomach. All of Jenny's dreams, gone up in flames. "What will Mr. Holloway do?"

"I'm not certain. I'm going to beg him to rebuild. This place is such a wonderful idea. And it's so needed. Don't you agree?"

"It's meant the world to me," Katie said, a hoarseness in her voice.

"One strange thing happened," Kimbra said. "During the fire, the portrait of Jenny fell. The frame shattered, but the canvas only suffered smoke damage. It can be cleaned and restored."

Katie felt good about that. Mr. Holloway loved the portrait so much. "Someone must have been watching over it."

Kimbra looked heavenward. "Someone was."

Lacey cleared her throat. "We'd like to take one last ride on the horses and we want Dullas to come with us. Do you think that'll be okay?"

Dullas started to protest, but Lacey silenced her with a look.

"I know DJ's down at the stables. He isn't flying out until tomorrow," Chelsea said.

"I'm not sure—" Kimbra said hesitantly.

"Oh, please," Katie begged. "We won't be gone but about an hour."

"I'll stay with Kimbra," Dullas announced.

"No, it's all right. You all go on," Kimbra told them. She nudged Dullas toward the stables. "I saw Richard's car in the parking lot and I have some things to talk over with him. You girls don't need to be hanging around these ruins."

Katie grabbed Dullas's hand and started for the stables. "See you soon," she called.

"Hey, let me go. I don't want to ride a stupid horse. I don't want to go any place with you all."

"There's something we want you to see," Lacey said. Then she added, "Please."

Dullas eyed her warily but didn't make a fuss.

DJ saddled up four horses without asking questions, yet he looked very curious as they rode off.

They rode quickly up the mountain trail to the familiar plateau. Chelsea didn't complain once, although her horse was trotting much faster than she would have liked. At the crest, they dismounted, tied their horses to trees, and went the rest of the way on foot. Atop the flat rock, Lacey turned to Dullas and gestured to the panoramic view of the tree-studded valley. "What do you think?"

Dullas looked bewildered. She lifted her chin defiantly. "Am I going to have an accident—you know, fall off the side or something?"

"Very funny." Lacey took a deep breath. "I'm sorry, okay! I should have never accused you of starting the fire."

"No lie."

"I had reason to be suspicious, you know. All last week, you treated people so mean. You made Latika cry, you said you hated me and hated Jenny House. Why did you act that way?"

Dullas stared down at the ground and kicked at a clump of earth with the toe of her sneaker. "You were talking about leaving . . . going home, and I didn't want to leave, that's all. I—I like it here and I knew I didn't have any place to go once the summer was over."

"Well, now you have a home to go to," Chelsea said.

Lacey led Dullas over to the tepee of sticks still standing in the rocks she'd piled at its base. "We built this a year ago. Added to it in November."

"What is it?"

"It's a memorial to Amanda and Jillian, but it's time to take it down."

"Why?"

"Because their true memorial is inside of us," Katie said, placing her hand over her heart. "Because their memory is what we have to share with others."

"Won't you come back next summer if Mr. Holloway fixes up Jenny House?"

"I'm going off to college," Katie said.

"My parents are planning to take me on a trip to Europe," Chelsea added.

"And I never plan too far in advance," Lacey finished. "So that leaves you to carry on."

"Carry on what?"

"Hope. Like Jillian wanted. Like Jenny Crawford wanted."

"But what if Jenny House is gone forever?"

"Don't you understand?" Katie asked. "Jenny House isn't so much a place as it is a feeling. An attitude of the heart. What matters is what we do with our lives, what we give to others."

Lacey reached down and untied the fluttering photo. "You're in charge of this now." She carefully plucked the earring from the photo. "We want you to take special care of it." She handed it to Dullas.

"Is it a real diamond?" Dullas's eyes grew round.

"It's from the crown of a fairy princess," Chelsea said. "Guard it."

Dullas glanced from face to face, as if they were playing some elaborate trick and might start laughing. When they didn't laugh, she asked, "You're serious? You want *me* to take care of a real diamond?"

"That's right. We're entrusting it to you for safe-keeping."

"Until when?"

Lacey offered a smile. "Until you find somebody you want to entrust it to."

"But who?"

"You'll know when you meet her," Katie said. "Just like we did."

"What if I get sick again?"

"You'll know what to do with it when the time comes," Lacey assured her.

For the first time in days, Dullas dropped her guard. She nodded, clutched the diamond stud tightly, and solemnly hugged each girl, first Chelsea, then Katie, and finally Lacey. "Will you write me at Kimbra's?" she asked.

"We'll write," Lacey said.

One of the horses whinnied impatiently. "We'd better go," Chelsea said. "I sure don't want that animal angry with me because he missed lunch."

They laughed together, then arm in arm walked to their horses and rode the trail down to all that remained of Jenny House.

Dear Reader,

For those of you who have been longtime readers, I hope you have enjoyed this One Last Wish volume. For those of you discovering One Last Wish for the first time, I hope you will want to read the other books that are listed in detail in the next few pages. From Lacey to Katie to Morgan and the rest, you'll discover the lives of the characters I hope you've come to care about just as I have.

Since the series began, I have received numerous letters from teens wishing to volunteer at Jenny House. That is not possible because Jenny House exists only in my imagination, but there are many fine organizations and camps for sick kids that would welcome volunteers. If you are interested in becoming such a volunteer, contact your local hospitals about their volunteer programs or try calling service organizations in your area to find out how you can help. Your own school might have a list of community service programs.

Extending yourself is one of the best ways of expanding your world . . . and of enlarging your heart. Turning good intentions into actions is consistently one of the most rewarding experiences in life. My wish is that the ideals of Jenny House will be carried on by you, my reader. I hope that now that we share the Jenny House attitude, you will believe as I do that the end is often only the beginning.

Thank you for caring.

YOU'LL WANT TO READ ALL THE ONE LAST WISH
BOOKS BY BESTSELLING AUTHOR

Let Him Live
Someone Dies, Someone Lives
Mother, Help Me Live
A Time to Die
Sixteen and Dying
Mourning Song
The Legacy: Making Wishes Come True
Please Don't Die
She Died Too Young
All the Days of Her Life
A Season for Goodbye
Reach for Tomorrow

$\mathcal{I}$F YOU WANT TO KNOW MORE ABOUT MEGAN,

BE SURE TO READ

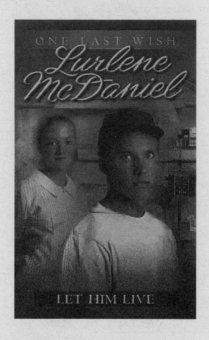

ON SALE NOW FROM BANTAM BOOKS
0-553-56067-0

Excerpt from *Let Him Live* by Lurlene McDaniel
Copyright © 1993 by Lurlene McDaniel

Published by Bantam Doubleday Dell Books for Young Readers
a division of Random House, Inc.
1540 Broadway, New York, New York 10036

*B*eing a candy striper isn't Megan Charnell's idea of an exciting summer, but she volunteered and can't get out of it. Megan has her own problems to deal with. Still, when she meets Donovan Jacoby, she find herself getting involved in his life.

Donovan shares with Megan his secret: An anonymous benefactor has granted him one last wish, and he needs Megan's help. The money can't buy a compatible transplant, but it can allow Donovan to give his mother and little brother something he feels he owes them. Can Megan help make his dream come true?

"When I first got sick in high school, kids were pretty sympathetic, but the sicker I got and the more school I missed, the harder it was to keep up with the old crowd," Donovan explained. *"Some of them tried to understand what I was going through, but unless you've been really sick . . ."* He didn't finish the sentence.

"I've never been sick," Meg said, *"but I really do know what you're talking about."*

He tipped his head and looked into her eyes. "I believe you do."

$\mathcal{J}$F YOU WANT TO KNOW MORE ABOUT

KATIE AND JOSH, BE SURE TO READ

ON SALE NOW FROM BANTAM BOOKS
0-553-29842-9

Excerpt from *Someone Dies, Someone Lives* by Lurlene McDaniel
Copyright © 1992 by Lurlene McDaniel

Published by Bantam Doubleday Dell Books for Young Readers
a division of Random House, Inc.
1540 Broadway, New York, New York 10036

$\mathcal{K}$atie O'Roark feels miserable, though she knows she's incredibly lucky to have received an anonymous gift of money. The money can't buy the new heart she needs or bring back her days as a track star.

A donor is found with a compatible heart, and Katie undergoes transplant surgery. While recuperating, she meets Josh Martel and senses an immediate connection. When Katie decides to start training to realize her dream of running again, Josh helps her meet the difficult challenge.

Will Katie find the strength physically and emotionally to live and become a winner again?

From the corner of her eye, Katie saw a boy with red hair who was about her age. He stood near the doorway, looking nervous. With a start, she realized he was watching her because he kept averting his gaze when she glanced his way. Odd, Katie told herself. Katie had a nagging sense she couldn't place him. As nonchalantly as possible, she rolled her wheelchair closer, picking up a magazine as she passed a table.

She flipped through the magazine, pretending to be interested, all the while glancing discreetly toward the boy. Even though he also picked up a magazine, Katie could tell that he was preoccupied with studying her. Suddenly, she grew self-conscious. Was something wrong with the way she looked? She'd thought she looked better than she had in months when she'd left her hospital room that afternoon. Why was he watching her?

Katie is also featured in the novels *Please Don't Die, She Died Too Young,* and *A Season for Goodbye.*

𝒯F YOU WANT TO KNOW MORE ABOUT SARAH,

BE SURE TO READ

ON SALE NOW FROM BANTAM BOOKS
0-553-29811-9

Excerpt from *Mother, Help Me Live* by Lurlene McDaniel
Copyright © 1992 by Lurlene McDaniel

Published by Bantam Doubleday Dell Books for Young Readers
a division of Random House, Inc.
1540 Broadway, New York, New York 10036

$\mathcal{S}$arah McGreggor is distraught when she learns she will need a bone marrow transplant to live. And she is shocked to find out that her parents and siblings can't be donors because they aren't her blood relatives. Sarah never knew she was adopted.

As Sarah faces this devastating news, she is granted one last wish by an anonymous benefactor. With hope in her heart, she begins a search for her birth mother, who gave her up fifteen years ago. Sarah's life depends on her finding this woman. But what will Sarah discover about the true meaning of family?

Didn't the letter from JWC say she could spend it on anything she wanted? What could be more important than finding her birth mother? What could be more important than discovering if she had siblings with compatible bone marrow? Her very life could depend on finding these people. Sarah practically jumped up from the sofa. "I've got to go," she said.

$\mathcal{I}$f you want to know more about Eric,

be sure to read

On Sale Now from Bantam Books
0-553-29809-7

Excerpt from *A Time to Die* by Lurlene McDaniel
Copyright © 1992 by Lurlene McDaniel

Published by Bantam Doubleday Dell Books for Young Readers
a division of Random House, Inc.
1540 Broadway, New York, New York 10036

*S*ixteen-year-old Kara Fischer has never considered herself lucky. She doesn't understand why she was born with cystic fibrosis. Despite her daily treatments, each day poses the threat of a lung infection that could put her in the hospital for weeks. But her close friendship with her fellow CF patient Vince and the new feelings she is quickly developing for Eric give her the hope to live one day at a time.

When an anonymous benefactor promises to grant a single wish with no strings attached, Kara finds a way to let the people who have loved and supported her throughout her illness know how much they mean to her. But will there be time for Kara to see her dying wish fulfilled?

"What am I going to do about you, Kara?"

Eric's tone was subdued and so sincere that his question caught her by surprise. "What do you mean?"

"I can't stay away from you."

"You seem to be doing a fine job of it," she said quietly, but without malice.

"I know it seems that way, but you don't know how hard it's been."

She was skeptical. "We just danced together, but after tonight, how will it be between us? Will you still ignore me in the halls? Will you duck into the nearest open door whenever you see me coming?"

He turned his head and she saw his jaw clench. She thought he might walk away, but instead he asked, "What's between you and Vince?"

$\mathcal{I}$F YOU WANT TO KNOW MORE ABOUT MORGAN,

BE SURE TO READ

ON SALE NOW FROM BANTAM BOOKS
0-553-29932-8

Excerpt from *Sixteen and Dying* by Lurlene McDaniel
Copyright © 1992 by Lurlene McDaniel

Published by Bantam Doubleday Dell Books for Young Readers
a division of Random House, Inc.
1540 Broadway, New York, New York 10036

$\mathcal{J}$t's hard for Anne Wingate and her father to accept the doctors' diagnosis: Anne is HIV-positive. Seven years ago, before blood screening was required, Anne received a transfusion. It saved her life then, but now the harsh reality can't be changed—the blood was tainted. Anne must deal with the inevitable progression of her condition.

When an anonymous benefactor promises to grant Anne a single wish with no strings attached, she decides to spend the summer on a ranch out west. She wants to live as normally as she possibly can. The summer seems even better than she dreamed, especially after she meets Morgan. Anne doesn't confide in Morgan about her condition and doesn't plan to. Then her health begins to deteriorate and she returns home. Is there time for Anne and Morgan to meet again?

Fearfully, Anne stared at her bleeding hand.

Morgan reached beneath her, lifted her, and placed her safely away from the hay and its invisible weapon. "Let me see how bad you're cut."

"It's nothing," Anne said, keeping her hand close to her body. "I'm fine."

"You're not fine. You're bleeding. You may need stitches. Let me wipe it off and examine it."

Her eyes widened, reminding him of a deer trapped in headlights. "No! Don't touch it!"

"But—"

"Please—you don't understand. I—I can't explain. Just don't touch it." Wild-eyed, panicked, she spun, and clutching her hand to her side, she bolted from the barn.

Dumbfounded, Morgan watched her run back toward the cabin.

$\mathcal{Y}$OU MAY ALSO WANT TO READ

ON SALE NOW FROM BANTAM BOOKS
0-553-29810-0

Excerpt from *Mourning Song* by Lurlene McDaniel
Copyright © 1992 by Lurlene McDaniel

Published by Bantam Doubleday Dell Books for Young Readers
a division of Random House, Inc.
1540 Broadway, New York, New York 10036

*I*t's been months since Dani Vanoy's older sister, Cassie, was diagnosed as having a brain tumor. And now the treatments aren't helping. Dani is furious that she is powerless to help her sister. She can't even convince their mother to take the girls on the trip to Florida Cassie has always longed for.

Then Cassie receives an anonymous letter offering her a single wish. Dani knows she can never make Cassie well, but she is determined to see Cassie's dream come true, with or without their mother's approval.

Dani had rehearsed the speech so many times that even she was beginning to believe it. "It's as if you're supposed to do this. While we don't know who gave you the money for a wish, I think you should use it to get something you've always wanted. Listen, even a trillion dollars can't make you well, but the money you've gotten can help you have some fun. I say let's go for it! You deserve to see the ocean, whether Mom agrees or not. I'm going to help you make your wish come true."

$\mathcal{I}$F YOU WANT TO KNOW MORE ABOUT RICHARD
HOLLOWAY AND JENNY CRAWFORD,

BE SURE TO READ

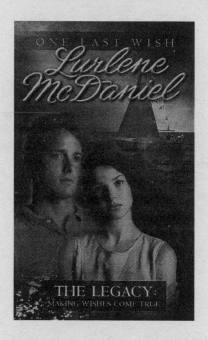

ON SALE NOW FROM BANTAM BOOKS
0-553-56134-0

Excerpt from *The Legacy: Making Wishes Come True* by Lurlene McDaniel
Copyright © 1993 by Lurlene McDaniel

Published by Bantam Doubleday Dell Books for Young Readers
a division of Random House, Inc.
1540 Broadway, New York, New York 10036

*W*ho is JWC, and how was the One Last Wish Foundation created? Follow JWC's struggle for survival against impossible odds and the intertwining stories of love and friendship that developed into a legacy of giving. And discover the power that one individual's determination can have, in this extraordinary novel of hope.

"I had my physician call the ER doctor and afterward, when we discussed their conversation, he suggested that I get her to a specialist as quickly as possible."

"A specialist at Boston Children's," Richard said with a nod. "What kind of specialist?"

"A pediatric oncologist."

Before Richard could say another word, Jenny's grandmother spoke. "A cancer specialist," Marian said, her voice catching. "They believe Jenny has leukemia."

$\mathcal{I}$F YOU WANT TO KNOW MORE ABOUT KATIE,

CHELSEA, AND LACEY,

BE SURE TO READ

ON SALE NOW FROM BANTAM BOOKS
0-553-56262-2

Excerpt from *Please Don't Die* by Lurlene McDaniel
Copyright © 1993 by Lurlene McDaniel

Published by Bantam Doubleday Dell Books for Young Readers
a division of Random House, Inc.
1540 Broadway, New York, New York 10036

*W*hen Katie O'Roark receives an invitation from the One Last Wish Foundation to spend the summer at Jenny House, she eagerly says yes. Katie is ever grateful to JWC, the unknown person who gave her the gift that allowed her to receive a heart transplant. Now Katie is asked to be a "big sister" to others who, like her, face daunting medical problems: Amanda, a thirteen-year-old victim of leukemia; Chelsea, a fourteen-year-old candidate for a heart transplant; and Lacey, a sixteen-year-old diabetic who refuses to deal with her condition. As the summer progresses, the girls form close bonds and enjoy the chance to act "just like healthy kids." But when a crisis jeopardizes one girl's chance of fulfilling her dreams, they discover true friendship and its power to endure beyond this life.

"Me, too. I don't know what I'd do without you, Katie. Whenever I think about last summer, about how you were so close to dying . . ."

She didn't allow him to complete his sentence. "Every day is new, every morning, Josh. I'm glad I got a second chance at life. And after meeting the people here at Jenny House, after making friends with Amanda, Chelsea, and even Lacey, I want all of us to live forever."

He grinned. "Forever's a long time."

She returned his smile. "All right, then at least until we're all old and wrinkled."

If YOU WANT TO KNOW MORE ABOUT
KATIE AND CHELSEA, BE SURE TO READ

ON SALE NOW FROM BANTAM BOOKS
0-553-56263-0

Excerpt from *She Died Too Young* by Lurlene McDaniel
Copyright © 1994 by Lurlene McDaniel

Published by Bantam Doubleday Dell Books for Young Readers
a division of Random House, Inc.
1540 Broadway, New York, New York 10036

*C*helsea James and Katie O'Roark met at Jenny House and spent a wonderful summer together.

Now Chelsea and her mother are staying with Katie as Chelsea awaits news about a heart transplant. While waiting for a compatible donor, Chelsea meets Jillian, a kind, funny girl who's waiting for a heart-lung transplant. The two girls become fast friends. When Chelsea meets Jillian's brother, he awakens feelings in her she's never known before. But as her medical situation grows desperate, Chelsea finds herself in a contest for her life against her best friend. Is it fair that there's a chance for only one of them to survive?

"Don't you see? There's one donor coming in. Only one. Who will the doctors save? Who will get the transplant?"

For a moment Josh stared blankly as her question sank in. "Katie, you don't know for sure there's only one donor."

"Yes, I do. There's only one. One heart. Two lungs. The doctor said the donor's family had given permission for all her organs to be donated." Katie's voice had risen with the tide of panic rising in her. "There's two people in need and only one heart."

Katie and Chelsea are also featured in the novels *Please Don't Die* and *A Season for Goodbye*.

*I*F YOU WANT TO KNOW MORE ABOUT LACEY,

BE SURE TO READ

ONE LAST WISH

Lurlene McDaniel

ALL THE DAYS
OF HER LIFE

ON SALE NOW FROM BANTAM BOOKS
0-553-56264-9

Excerpt from *All the Days of Her Life* by Lurlene McDaniel
Copyright © 1994 by Lurlene McDaniel

Published by Bantam Doubleday Dell Books for Young Readers
a division of Random House, Inc.
1540 Broadway, New York, New York 10036

Out of control—that's how Lacey Duval feels in almost every aspect of her life. There's nothing she can do about her parents' divorce, there's nothing she can do about the death of her young friend, there's nothing she can do about having diabetes—that's what Lacey believes.

After a special summer at Jenny House, Lacey is determined to put her problems behind her. When she returns to high school, she is driven to become a part of the in crowd. But Lacey thinks fitting in means losing weight and hiding her diabetes. She starts skipping meals and experimenting with her medication—sometimes ignoring it altogether.

Her friends from the summer caution her to face her problems before catastrophe strikes. Is it too late to stop the destructive process Lacey has set in motion?

She went hot and cold all over. It was as if he'd shone a light into some secret part of her heart and something dark and ugly had crawled out. She had rejected Jeff because she didn't want a sick boyfriend. She'd said as much to Katie at Jenny House.

"It's any sickness, Jeff. It's mine too. I hate it all. I know it's not your fault, but it's not mine either."

"I'll bet no one at your school knows you're a diabetic."

She said nothing.

"I'm right, aren't I?"

"It's none of your business."

"You know, Lacey, you're the person who won't accept that you have a disease. Why is that?"

She whirled on him. "How can you ask me that when you've just admitted that girls drop you once they discover you're a bleeder? You of all people should understand why I keep my little secret."

Lacey is also featured in the novels *Please Don't Die* and *A Season for Goodbye*.

IF YOU WANT TO KNOW MORE ABOUT KATIE,
CHELSEA, AND LACEY, BE SURE TO READ

ON SALE NOW FROM BANTAM BOOKS
0-553-56265-7

Excerpt from *A Season for Goodbye* by Lurlene McDaniel
Copyright © 1995 by Lurlene McDaniel

Published by Bantam Doubleday Dell Books for Young Readers
a division of Random House, Inc.
1540 Broadway, New York, New York 10036

*T*ogether again. It's been a year since Katie O'Roark, Chelsea James, and Lacey Duval shared a special summer at Jenny House. The girls have each spent the year struggling to fit into the world of the healthy. Now they're back, this time as "big sisters" to a new group of girls who also face life-threatening illnesses.

But even as the friends strive to help their "little sisters" face the future together, they must separately confront their own expectations. Katie must decide between an old flame and an exciting scholarship far from home. Chelsea must overcome her fear of romance. And Lacey must convince the boy she loves that her feelings for him can be trusted.

When tragedy strikes Jenny House, each of the girls knows that things can never be the same. Will Lacey, Chelsea, and Katie find a way to carry on the legacy of Jenny House? Can their special friendship endure?

"Over here!" Katie called. "I found it."

Chelsea and Lacey hurried to where Katie was crouched, digging through a pile of dead leaves. The tepee was partially buried, and Chelsea held her breath, hoping that the laminated photo and Jillian's diamond stud earring were still tied to it.

"It's come apart," Katie said, lifting up the twigs in three parts. But from the corner of one of the sticks, the laminated photo dangled, and from its center the diamond caught the afternoon sunlight.

The photo looked faded, but Amanda still smiled from the center of their group. Chelsea felt a lump form in her throat. These days, she and Katie and Lacey looked older, more mature, healthier too. But Amanda looked the same, her gamine smile frozen in time. And ageless.

Katie took the photo from Lacey's trembling fingers. "We were quite a bunch, weren't we?"

*Y*OU CAN READ MORE ABOUT
MANY OF YOUR FAVORITE CHARACTERS FROM
THE ONE LAST WISH BOOKS IN

ON SALE NOW FROM BANTAM BOOKS
0-553-57109-5

Excerpt from *Reach for Tomorrow* by Lurlene McDaniel
Copyright © 1999 by Lurlene McDaniel

Published by Bantam Doubleday Dell Books for Young Readers
a division of Random House, Inc.
1540 Broadway, New York, New York 10036

*K*atie O'Roark is thrilled to learn that Jenny House is being rebuilt. After the fire last year, Katie thought she could never return to the camp, where she spent the summers with young men and women like her who faced medical odds that were stacked against them. But thanks to Richard Holloway's efforts, Katie and her longtime friends Lacey and Chelsea will work as counselors once again. They'll be joined by Megan Charnell, Morgan Lancaster, and Eric Lawrence, who are newcomers to Jenny House but who have experienced the generosity of the One Last Wish Foundation.

It's not until Katie arrives at camp that she discovers that Josh Martel, her former boyfriend, is also a counselor. Katie and Josh broke up a year ago, when Katie decided to go away to college. Being near Josh again brings back a flood of old emotions for Katie. And when Josh confronts unexpected adversity, Katie knows she has to work out her feelings for him. Through the heart transplant she underwent years ago, Katie miraculously received a gift of new life. Now she must discover how to make the most of that precious gift and choose her future.

She stopped. By now tears had filled her eyes and her heart felt as if it might break. She truly believed that God had heard her prayer. What she did not know was whether or not he would grant her request. Against great odds, God had given her a new heart when she'd desperately needed one. And he had brought Josh into her life as well. She believed that with all her heart and soul. Now there was nothing more she could do except wait. And have faith.

Katie lifted her arms in the moonlight in supplication to the heavens.

*B*e my angel . . .

Special hardcover edition!

ISBN: 0-553-57145-1

*H*eather is unprepared to face the famine and misery she encounters when she joins a mission group. Only Ian, a medical volunteer, can help her see beyond the horror in this inspirational new novel from bestselling author Lurlene McDaniel.

DO WISHES COME TRUE WHEN YOU WISH UPON A STAR?

ISBN: 0-553-57130-3

You won't want to miss Lurlene McDaniel's special hardcover edition featuring three heartwarming and inspirational novellas that capture the true spirit of the holiday season.